D0197894

IT'S NOT JUST ABOUT RAIN

A.L.Smith

ISBN: 978-1-4834-5462-7 (sc)
ISBN: 978-1-4834-5463-4 (e)

Lulu Publishing Services rev. date: 7/21/2016

WEATHER FORECAST

This is the fourth book in the series written as a tribute to those 'wonders of Wythenshawe' that deliver a combination of weather, some ordered, some not.

'Making Rain and Other Things Is Our Business' introduced readers to the crew of the Nimbus and provided an insight into their world of weather. 'A Cloud's Life' elaborated on their work and 'Weather to Order' continued describing the climate they interfere with.

Drizzling to order, topping up reservoirs and providing showers may not seem particularly unique weather activities but when you learn the reasons for doing it, you may be most surprised.

What could be the connection between Clitheroe's persistent mist and Wythenshawe's wonders? The Clitheroe Constabulary was faced with a mystifying crime, but solve it they did.

Everything has a beginning and the world of weather-making is no exception. Hitler had a part to play in it and the story is revealed in Salford's Cloud Museum.

Nothing in this world stands still, not even a cloud. Black, Black & Blackemore's in deeper Salford, the only cloud machine manufacturer in existence, are constantly faced with new and bigger challenges – 'Cloudtanic' being one of them.

When a hundred or so cloud machines are busy delivering weather around the globe there is always the chance that the paths of one or two will cross and not all result in a happy ending.

In a world troubled so much by strife in one form or another it's a relief to discover that romance is in the air, and it is! Weddings, honeymoons, a plan for a couple madly in love with each other – it's all part of the rich heritage of Wythenshawe Weather Centre and long may it continue.

I dedicate this book to all those who are driven insane by the changeable UK weather but I accept no responsibility for it. When I step outside my front door I take the same weather risk as the rest of you, irrespective of whether it's from Wythenshawe or one of nature's wondrous jobs. Like you, I can't differentiate between man-made and natural rain; they both soak me. For sharing this insanity, I can only offer two pieces of advice: invest in an umbrella manufacturer and keep smiling!

CONTENTS

Maps

PREFACE

Background to the Stories

The concept of a weather-making industry had its origins in my mind in 1985 and was originally conceived to entertain children – Dutch children to be precise. Twenty-five years later, I returned to the concept but this time with much older children (adults) in mind. Well, we all get rained on!

My first book – **Making Rain and Other Things Is Our Business!** – takes the reader from those early beginnings, to the modern day hurly-burly of making rain and other things. My second – **A Cloud's Life** – continued the revelations. **Weather to Order** – illustrated some of the history of weather-making and its progressive development.

It's Not Just About Rain – is the fourth book on the subject of weather solutions. I'm not sure how I got this far but the journey on a whim and a wind was fascinating!

Rain and clouds, we all know, are connected but tales of mysterious weather abound and within the pages of this book I reveal the truth about 'the desperate drizzle' and 'gambling on a shower'.

To prove it's not all about rain you will discover the connection between clouds and watercress and the grand solution to the melting ice caps.

Crime, unfortunately, extends into everything and the world of weather-making is no exception and once upon a time the town of Clitheroe felt the results in a frustratingly foggy way.

Romance plays its part in the skies above us and not just between the individuals who crew the machines that provide weather solutions. To say that 'love is in the air' is not an exaggeration.

The process of delivering weather can be a hazardous business and is not accident free, as you will learn.

For those of you who are historically minded, here is an opportunity to learn about the origins of cloud making. Hitler would have shaken in his boots if he had known about it!

Enjoy the journey, but I must leave you now, I have a cloud to catch.

Tony Smith
September 18th, 2014

ACKNOWLEDGEMENTS

As with my first three books, 'Making Rain and Other Things Is Our Business!', 'A Cloud's Life' and 'Weather to Order', this latest gem of rain-making could not have been created without the help of three particular people. My neighbour, Helen, cast an eye over my work and swept up commas and punctuation marks that were being used inappropriately before putting them where they should have been. Andy Cooper from Draw & Code Ltd did the front cover using his considerable artistic talent. My friend Eddie Challoner drew some illustrations for me before departing, shaking his head as he went. They all know I don't like grapes and I hope they remember when they come to visit me.

INTRODUCTION

Anyone who has read my books, 'Making Rain and Other Things Is Our Business', 'A Cloud's Life' and 'Weather to Order' will be well versed in the variety of weather solutions provided by the cloud machines that operate from Wythenshawe Weather Centre. However, the variety is of such magnitude that there is still much to tell.

The British tend not be comfortable with long dry summers at home; it always generates frustration amongst a society geared to a more changeable climate. A long hot summer in Scarborough led to the town council hiring a drizzle to bring some normality back to the place and quell any trouble from agitated holidaymakers. Oban's 'Fresh Food Gathering' was in danger of displaying distinctly lack-lustre watercress unless the current drought could be alleviated, and steps were taken to do just that. Great Yarmouth's long tradition of 'slot machines' was given a fillip by creating a jackpot shower.

A visit to the Cloud Museum in deeper Salford reveals more of the history of weather-making which had its origins in military work in World War II. Post-war development was initially slow but the last couple of decades have seen a dramatic evolution.

Crime extends to all sectors of society and the world of weather is no exception. There are always victims and the population of Clitheroe became just that when they were afflicted by a persistent mist that no-one had forecast and it seemed to last forever.

Delivering weather solutions is not free from risk and when cloud machine operatives don't stick to strict procedures it is inevitable that something will go wrong, as was witnessed in Peel on the Isle-of-Man.

Romance is universal and the sky is not 'off-limits'. The parents of two amorous young undergraduates went to great lengths to minimize their opportunity to fraternize during a long summer break and the weather world provided the solution. At the opposite end of the romance scale, a honeymoon cruise onboard a suitably modified cloud machine was a dream come true for an American couple with Scottish connections. Romance doesn't simply extend to folk outside the weather-making world. It has its own love stories to tell and none more so than the 'will they, won't they' couple that meet infrequently in Slaidburn.

You can enjoy all this stuff without getting wet, but it would still be advisable to have an umbrella handy – better to be safe rather than drenched!

THE STOLEN DRIP

C irrus Cumulus was busy killing ants to musical accompaniment at his Slaidburn home whilst his faithful engineer, Puffy White, watched in amusement from a distance. Cirrus hated ants with a vengeance and especially those that appeared in his drive every summer. In spite of the liberal sprinklings of ant powder he regularly put down, it didn't seem to prevent the annual invasion of the blighters. Ants were an obsession of Cirrus's and immediately on sight of one on his drive he would rush outside and stamp on them. The problem was, no sooner had he stamped on one than he saw another and stamping continued, but not always in the same place or on the same foot. From the outside, any spectator would be mystified by the process which looked like either a tribal dance or some new form of physical exercise. Whichever it was, it did no good for the ants but they still came back for more each year.

Killing ants was developed into a fine art by Cirrus, or perhaps that should be a fine dance. To make the business of killing more palatable, Cirrus would play one of his favourite Brass Band Cds. With the lounge window open, the sound carried nicely over his drive not to mention most of the village as well, and stamping on ants to the accompaniment of Brass was highly entertaining unless you were an ant.

Slaidburn village community had got accustomed to the two cloud machine operatives living amongst them and were well acquainted with most of their odd and eccentric habits. They knew by now that when loud Brass music came from the Aurora Cloudealis, which was the name of the Cumulus home, Cirrus would be performing his ant-killing dance. They knew because they had been to watch him and applauded his unique style, even if it lacked grace and did nothing in terms of Slaidburn's total ant population.

A waft of bacon would signal mid morning refreshments and Cirrus would break off from his killing spree and make his way indoors to enjoy the fruits, or to be more accurate, the bacon butties and coffee, of his engineer's cooking.

"Good morning, Captain. I thought you needed a break after all that exertion. I've brought you a copy of the paper as well."

"Thanks, Puffy. I'm just ready for that. By the way, I think we need to get another lot of ant powder."

"Leave that to me, skipper."

At that point Puffy left his Captain to enjoy his refreshments whilst hoping at the same time that there was nothing in the newspaper that would induce any passionate feelings in him. The Daily Gloom had a tendency to highlight all the dismal aspects of life and the inadequacies of the society that inherits the Globe, although Cirrus tended to focus more on the society that inherits the UK. That apart, if anything appeared that his skipper didn't like it would mean that he was going to get his ear bent at some point during the day, so he'd better be on his guard.

Puffy retreated to the kitchen and waited for the inevitable. After thirty minutes it was time to face his Captain and collect what crockery needed washing. He walked down the hall and tapped on the lounge door before entering. It was not needed but old habits die hard. With a degree of caution, he entered the room and whilst his skipper continued reading he collected the crockery and started to make his way out.

"This damned hacking business is really depressing."

Now for it, thought Puffy.

"All this high technology stuff is all very fine but it seems all too easy for the bad guys to use it to their advantage. Just look at the intelligence stuff that private

individuals are finding access to and then using it to create mischief. Nobody can have any secrets anymore, at least not on a computer."

Puffy nodded in agreement, simply hoping that this was not going to be a prolonged outburst of Cirrus's views on things.

"It really makes you worry about people gaining access into your own computer and 'hacking' as they call it. You know, I read that some people who have internet banking have had their banking details stolen and have had money taken from their accounts without being aware of it."

"That's pretty scary, Captain. Isn't there such a thing as a firewall that you can install on your computer to stop anyone gaining access to what's on your computer?"

Cirrus looked up at Puffy, partly in disbelief that he would know this and partly because he had just spotted a rabbit running across the lawn outside, but it didn't stop him from returning to the subject of hacking.

"That's so but that doesn't seem to stop everybody. Those with a degree of knowledge in these matters still seem to get round whatever precautions are taken. Lets face it, if National Security establishments can get hacked, what hope is there for the rest of us?"

Puffy had picked up the dirty crockery and started for the lounge door.

"And I'll tell you something else that's positively dodgy."

Realising that he wasn't going to get away that easily, Puffy braced himself for the next onslaught of his skipper's views.

"Look at the way all these social media sites are being used to abuse people. Why on earth does anyone want to expose themselves to that risk? Youngsters in particular are too inclined to have conversations with people they don't know and give away all kinds of inappropriate information about themselves."

"I agree with you there skipper, and some people using these sites use false identities to help them induce youngsters to give personal details away. It's pretty scary really."

"Well I can assure you that I'm not going to use one of these sites to talk to people. I'm going to stick to the tried and tested old fashioned ways, but I would be worried if I had kids."

A lull in the conversation provided Puffy with an opportunity to make for the door again and this time he made it and he closed it behind him.

Unusual News

The telephone rang and Cirrus answered it.

"Hello, Captain Cumulus speaking."

"Good morning, Captain. It's Miss Black here."

Miss Joanne Black was the secretary of Mr Spite CDM who was the Superintendent at Wythenshawe Weather Centre.

"Good morning, Goldilocks. What can I do for you?"

Cirrus could hear Miss Black chuckling to herself at being called Goldilocks but that was the nickname everyone working from the Weather Centre had for her.

"Mr Spite would like to speak to you. Is it convenient for you to do that or would you prefer to call back?"

"Put him through now please."

"I will do that, Captain, but before I do would you kindly thank Mr White for the box of chocolates he sent me. They were really nice?"

Mr Percival White, more commonly known as Puffy is the Flight Engineer on board the cloud machine, Nimbus which is piloted by Captain Cumulus.

I wonder what that rascal Puffy is up to, thought Cirrus, but before he could wonder much more, the voice of the Superintendent came on the phone.

"It's Spite here. Can you hear me Cirrus?"

"I can indeed Mr Spite. What can I do for you?"

"It's rather bizarre! The Drip's gone missing."

The Drip is a cloud machine that operates from Wythenshawe Weather Centre and is hangared there when not in use. The crew had been comprised of Arthur Treadmill and Larry Oliver until relatively recently. Arthur was serving a six month period of suspension as a result of being found guilty of sabotaging the Nimbus whilst it was engaged in providing overnight rain for the Chelsea Flower Show. The washing-up liquid that he had put into the water storage tanks of the Nimbus created huge bubbles over everything when the Nimbus rained, and the organisers had not been pleased. And they had not been appeased by the resultant cleanliness of everything. Arthur had committed this act of sabotage in order to discredit Cirrus in the eyes of Abigail Windrush and enhance his own prospects. Arthur was well known as a womaniser but not necessarily by his female victims.

Not long after being given a suspension, Arthur had met up with an Australian girl from Melbourne who had a share in a boomerang factory and he had emigrated there. In his absence his share of the Drip had passed to his Flight Engineer, Larry Oliver. It was only recently that Larry had recruited a new pilot, Oscar Blowhard, and after a lengthy period of inactivity and zero earnings, that he had finally found work. In addition to losing his share of the Drip, Arthur also lost his long suffering wife Lilly who had left him for one of his work colleagues, Bert Drummond. Bert was the Flight Engineer on the Discovery and held in high esteem by his skipper, Wally Lenticular.

"When you say the Drip's gone missing, what exactly do you mean? Has it disappeared on a job?"

"No no. I think it's been stolen."

"What makes you think that?"

"Larry Oliver turned up at Wythenshawe this morning and when he went into the hangar the Drip had gone."

"Has anyone reported it missing to the Police?"

"Larry did and it turned out to be quite an ordeal."

Mr Spite went on to describe how Larry had tried to report the missing Drip at the local Police Station. On arrival at the reporting desk, a burly Police Sergeant had enquired how he might be of help and when told by Larry that he wanted to report a missing cloud machine he looked at him with considerable disdain. Nevertheless, the sergeant picked up a pen and prepared himself to take down the details.

"And what does this cloud machine look like?"

Larry tried to explain that cloud machines are not allowed to be seen naked and therefore a description of it would not be relevant. Having jotted down a few comments, the sergeant looked up again.

"So how will we know when we have found it?"

Larry explained how a cloud machine creates a cloud around itself so that no-one can see it. The sergeant continued to jot things down before posing another question.

"So what does this missing cloud look like?"

Larry was clearly getting embarrassed trying to give an answer to these questions but tried to explain that cloud machines can create a whole variety of different clouds. The Drip could be any one of many different types. The sergeant put his pen down and then put one elbow on the desk to support a hand that held his chin aloft.

"Have you tried reporting this to the Met Office? They might be more helpful. They might have a missing cloud section."

Larry could sense a loss of interest by the desk sergeant but insisted that he continued filing a report.

"Where was this missing cloud last seen?"

This was much more straight forward to answer.

"Wythenshawe Weather Centre," replied Larry.

"When was it last seen?"

The Drip had been parked up in the hangar at Wythenshawe the night before but had gone by lunch time today. At this stage there was nothing else that could be said. The sergeant heaved a sigh of relief before saying, *"Leave this with us and we will make some enquiries, but it may be difficult for us to find it on the basis of the information you have provided."*

Larry had then left the Police Station feeling somewhat disheartened but noticed, as he was making his way back to the Weather Centre, that every Policeman he saw appeared to be looking, in a mystified way, at the sky above.

Conjecture

The telephone conversation then changed to the subject of who could have done it and why.

"The thing I can't get my head around, Cirrus, is why anyone would do this. The Drip couldn't take on any work without being found out. Everything goes through us at Wythenshawe."

"What about that chap in the Isle-of-Man?"

"You mean Vannin?"

"That's the chap."

"Well Vannin has been a bit of a rogue, I'll grant you that, but he is now an adviser in the Weather-Making Research Centre. He's hardly likely to jeopardise that. The only idea that I can think of is that someone has stolen it for a ransom or just purely for kicks. Either way, we will find out eventually."

It occurred to Cirrus that there could possibly be another reason and he needed to share it.

"I can't help wondering if this is down to Arthur Treadmill?"

"What makes you think that, Cirrus?"

"I know he felt pretty sore when he lost his share of the Drip."

"That may be so but if he got the Drip back he couldn't do anything with it."

"Maybe Arthur just wants to deny the use of it to Larry and Oscar but this is all conjecture. Maybe Larry should go back to the Police and see if they could check if Arthur is still in Australia."

"That's a good point. I'll get on to Larry."

Thoughts now moved to the fact that the theft could not have been achieved without some inside help.

"Somebody in the Weather Centre must have been in on this. Somebody must have tipped the thieves off about the best time to steal the Drip. They would have to do it when no-one was around. I will carry out some investigations and see what I can find out."

"There is another point, Mr Spite."

"What's that, Cirrus?"

"Whoever stole the Drip must be either a Pilot or Flight Engineer and whatever role they had they would need a second crew member to fly it."

"You are absolutely right. We do have a few things to investigate. I'll get on to it."

The call finally came to an end and, as it did so, Puffy came back into the lounge and Cirrus had pleasure in relating events to him before a new subject was embarked upon.

"By the way, Puffy, Goldilocks sends her thanks for the box of chocolates you sent her."

Cirrus waited for a reaction but Puffy struggled and shrugged before making some kind of a grunt and then exiting the lounge in a rather hurried fashion.

On The Banks of the Hodder

Abigail Windrush was the skipper of the cloud machine named Hurricane and, like Cirrus, she operated out of Wythenshawe. Her weather work came in an unpredictable form of drizzle and drops which meant that her life had little in the way of routine. One week it may be a downpour in Aberdeen, the next it could be cloud posing off the coast of Torquay, but whatever the weather was to be she would deliver it and in return she got paid. For Abigail, weather was a way of life as well as nature and making it she did with a passion.

Anyone involved in weather-making will tell you that there really isn't much time for romance and even if there was one needed to be careful if one wanted to avoid a watershed. No-one in the business would like to face making a choice between the weather or a partner. Life without rain or other things was unthinkable. Some in the business had succeeded in combining the two but many had run into a marital storm. This was the issue being faced by Abigail and Cirrus. Both loved the weather business and for the time being they had mutually agreed to keep their passions under control.

Cirrus had a fixation about the age difference between Abigail and himself. He couldn't avoid thinking that someone as young as she was should really be with someone younger than himself but, on the other hand, he felt privileged that she had feelings for him and he certainly enjoyed being with her. Abigail thought that the issue of age difference was nonsense and had no qualms about being with Cirrus. She was, however, aware that he was influenced about the well being of his Flight Engineer, Puffy, since the two had worked closely together and shared the house in Slaidburn for many years. She had no desire to come between these two cloud workers and indeed she liked both of them.

Whenever Abigail and Cirrus saw a break in weather work they invariably tried to get together, and that's exactly how they came to be strolling along the banks of the River Hodder as it meanders past the village of Slaidburn. The river in these parts snakes its curving way through delightfully green pastures that curve gently upwards on both sides to create a valley of

9

peace and tranquility. Trees and nature's own garden of flowers added to the scene whilst sheep nibbling at the grass played their own role in life's adventure. Under a blue cloudless sky, and how could it be anything else if Wythenshawe's machines were all temporarily redundant, it was a dream to be enjoying the air and each other and it was so intoxicating.

Cirrus cast his eyes along the riverside path that he and Abigail had walked before but somehow it felt different today. Whatever the ingredients that were creating today's experience, it felt good. Abigail looked most attractive in the simple dress that she wore. It showed off her curves and, when added to her flowing hair and natural good looks, she looked extremely desirable. They meandered on towards the village of Newton-in-Bowland chatting about this and that. A short break in conversation occurred and on a sudden impulse, most uncharacteristic of Cirrus, he placed one arm around her waist and drew her around to face him. Taking an admiring look at her face, Cirrus embraced Abigail and kissed her in a way he had never had the courage to do before.

After what seemed to be an eternity, the two parted lips and were left gazing at each other before Abigail returned the compliment. It was a local farmer who broke the pair up before their passion had progressed further, but the interruption gave them a chance to top up their oxygen levels. After pleasantries had been exchanged, the cloud couple headed back arm in arm to Slaidburn laughing as they went and embraced in a common feeling of human love.

Puffy was waiting to greet the pair as they returned to the Aurora Cloudealis which was the name he and Cirrus had endowed their home with. It was all too obvious from the glow that radiated from the two of them that they were in love and it engendered a feeling of well being in Puffy. He had a deep respect for his skipper and a desire that he would eventually find someone to share his life with. The fact that he was sharing his skipper's life did not concern him. If his skipper had found happiness, then that was ok by him. Once he had got the pair of them settled around the dining table and they had eaten, he skipped off to the pub and left them to it. Over a few pints he could drool on his thoughts about Goldilocks in Wythenshawe.

Reports come in

"Skipper, there's a call from Mr Spite," shouted Puffy.

Cirrus dropped what he was doing and picked up the phone in the lounge.

"Cirrus here! What can I do for you Mr Spite?"

"Good morning, Cirrus. I have just received an interesting report from the Police regarding Arthur Treadmill."

This sounded interesting and Puffy, who had been hanging around the half open lounge door hoping to catch something of the conversation, was spotted by Cirrus who silently beckoned him in.

"I'm all ears, Mr Spite."

"The bottom line is that Arthur has arrived back here in the UK. You remember that his wife, Lily, left him don't you?"

"She went off with Wally's Flight Engineer, Bert Drummond, didn't she?"

"That's right. Anyway, he met up with an Australian woman called Alison from Melbourne and she had a share in a boomerang factory. He went out to Australia with her but his eyes started to wander again. Evidently Alison discovered his philandering and hit him with a boomerang before kicking him out. She had three big brothers who sent him their regards on the end of three fists, and he left the country with several Australian bruises as souvenirs."

"Do the Police know where he is now?" asked Cirrus.

The Police didn't know where Arthur was at present but Mr Spite had provided them with an address in Clitheroe were Arthur had lived with Lily and they were going to investigate it.

"The other report I received today is from the Civil Aviation Authority. They are complaining about an unauthorised takeoff from the Weather Centre on the day the Drip was stolen. A jumbo jet was coming in to land at Manchester Airport and was making its final approach when, and I quote, a craft which looked like a space ship ascended vertically directly across their flight path.

The airliner, carrying over 300 passengers, had to abort the landing by taking evasive action in order to avoid a collision. Luckily the airliner was able to go around again and land safely."

"Did any of the passengers see the machine?"

None of the passengers aboard Flight NY2U from New York had seen anything. The rogue craft had ascended directly in front of the airliner and only the pilots had got a glimpse of it. The crew had filed a report on landing and then they had been breathalysed but the results were negative.

"All our records here at Wythenshawe have been looked at and we can't find any flight take off recorded on the date and time in question but there is no doubt it must have been the Drip."

"Do you know who was on duty at the time? That would seem to me to be the next thing to look at."

Mr Spite agreed and that's where things were left for the moment.

"Cirrus, it sounds as if there are a few lines of enquiry being followed up."

"It's Captain to you. Don't take liberties. However, you are correct Puffy. It will be interesting to see how things develop."

A few days later it was a report in the local press that caught the eye of Cirrus. The Clitheroe Reporter gave coverage about a mysterious mist that had remained settled over the north of the town for several days and there was no sign of it moving. Not even the local breeze had made any impact on it. Morning mists at this time of the year were not unusual but most tended to vanish by lunch time. This was very much a persistent mist and the locals were getting upset by it.

You can't hang washing out in a mist; it just doesn't dry in a mist. Go shopping with three kids and you come back with two, although some thought that that had some advantages. Crossing a busy road in a mist can be a hairy experience and, not infrequently, fists had been waved by pedestrians at motorists and visa versa. Driving a bus in these conditions is not much fun either. Sharp bends appear from nowhere, as do traffic lights, and its touch and go whether the driver spots all the bus stops. Not everyone arrived at where they wanted to be or got on the bus that would take them there.

There was clearly something wrong about a mist that wouldn't go away and the people from Clitheroe demanded an explanation. Who brought it and why? What is it in aid of? There's no placating a mystified population. Someone was responsible. Who runs nature anyway? If the Police didn't find a culprit soon there would be rioting in Clitheroe.

There had been a queue outside the local Police Station for several hours and a frustrated desk sergeant was having difficulty working out what was to be done. When all was said and done, the Police didn't have a mist investigation branch. What do you do about a persistent mist? They did try bringing in a large rotatable propeller on the back of a lorry, complete with its own propulsion system, but all it did was swirl the mist around and when the propeller ceased rotating it settled again. House to house enquiries were being made but what kind of a question do you ask in these circumstances: *Is this your mist? Well get it moved. Clitheroe has a ban on permanent mists.* Needless to say, enquiries were not yielding any results.

Upon reading this report Cirrus jumped out of his chair and shouted at Puffy.

"That's where Arthur lived with Lily. I'll bet Arthur is behind this and the Drip won't be far behind."

"But why has he not got rid of the cloud?" asked Puffy.

"I'll bet he has nowhere to store the Drip out of the public's view and keeping the cloud around it was the best he could do."

"Bless me Captain, I think you have something there!"

Cirrus passed his thoughts on to Mr Spite in Wythenshawe who in turn tried to contact the Clitheroe Police. It took several hours to get through to the Police Station as a result of the number being constantly engaged but he did eventually make contact. A local Bobby was dispatched on his bicycle to apprehend the cloud thief.

PC Upstart made his way on a bicycle to number 96, Thorogood Gardens through the thick, long-lasting mist, with the aid of a street map. The distance was not great but navigating was most difficult, and his journey was not done by the shortest route. On two occasions that he knew of he found himself cycling through the front gate of somebody's house but once extricated he got back on course.

Number 96 was an unspectacular end of row terraced house, not the sort of hideaway any self-respecting cloud thief would choose. It was impossible to see above the front door but the large knocker looked convenient and as all Police Officers do, it was knocked quite forcibly.

"Are you Mr Arthur Treadmill?"

"Who wants to know?"

It was not the kind of answer to give to a Policeman who had just navigated through a nerve-racking mist that on a few occasions had come close to costing him his manhood.

Pinned up against his own front door, Arthur's demeanor changed and he admitted that Arthur was his first name and egged on by a little more coercion, he also agreed that since birth his last name had been Treadmill but whether that came from his mother's side or his father's, he couldn't say.

"Is this mist yours?" asked the Officer, using the straight talk that they do.

"Don't be daft! How can any bloke own a mist?"

That answer foxed the Police Constable but after a moment he recovered from his thoughts and pressed on. Well actually he pressed on Arthur's chest but it did not elicit the response that he wanted.

"Arthur Treadmill, are you responsible for stealing this mist?"

Just as Arthur was about to give another flippant answer, the sound of several sirens blasted out through the mist and, in due course, Thorogood Gardens was flooded with highly coloured Police cars complete with blue flashing lights. An army of Police Officers using coloured language rushed for number 96 and, seeing all this, Arthur's valour disappeared into the mist and he responded to PC Upstarts last question.

"Yes, Officer. It was me. I stole this mist."

A superior Officer from Wythenshawe heading enquiries reached the front door of number 96 just as PC Upstart was releasing his grip on the mist thief. The local PC was however baffled by how anyone could steal a mist. Apart from that, why would anyone want to steal a mist? What could you do with a mist? It was all very mystifying!

Detective Inspector Rainer took over the questioning and rapidly established that the Drip was parked in the middle of the field behind number 96 and an army of Officers entered the mist to find it. It was unfortunate that no-one had had the sense to do a head count as they all disappeared into the murk. It is recorded that not all of them returned, but that's local folklore.

Groping around in a thick mist can result in surprises and not all of them were of a friendly nature. Try being a bull lost in a mist for a few days and you will get the picture. Cows and cow shit is an inevitable feature of many fields, but in a mist it's not always possible to see what you are putting your foot in and some of the field's contents were brought back into Thorogood Gardens complete with a free aroma; they come in a package deal. The Drip was found intact in the middle of the field.

Clitheroe had to endure its mist for a couple more days whilst engineers from Black, Black & Blackemores checked the Drip out. Finding everything in order, a volunteer crew from Wythenshawe arrived to fly it back and photographers gathered to watch it lift off into the sky, revealing as it did so the missing Police Officers, several kids and a few unsuspecting courting couples taking advantage of the cover. The next edition of the Clitheroe Reporter had a fabulous front page photo of a cloud but it was impossible to tell the significance of it without reading the headline –

The Clitheroe mist is finally lifted.

Charges are brought

Treadmill was brought to Court charged with theft, flying whilst being suspended and misting with intent. He pleaded guilty to the first two charges but pleaded extenuating circumstances to the latter. When asked to explain what the extenuating circumstances were he replied that he had intended to rain his mist, or cloud, off before landing and then hide the Drip in a disused barn on the edge of the field it had been found in. Unfortunately, his Flight Engineer, George Thickster, was not familiar with the procedure and hence the cloud or mist could not be condensed before landing. Pressed by the prosecution as to what he had intended to do when he discovered that, he replied that he went to the pub and forgot all about it.

Arthur Treadmill was found guilty on all three charges and George Thickster was found guilty of aiding and abetting. The presiding judge left the two guilty men under no illusion as to the severity of what they had done, with particular reference to the mist they had dumped on Clitheroe. In view of the terrible impact that living in a permanent mist had made on the poor townsfolk, the judge felt that it was imperative that they both be kept away from people for as long as it was necessary. They were sentenced to six months cleaning up seagull droppings on St.Kilda, an island situated 100 miles west of the Scottish Hebrides.

"Well, Cirrus, what do you think about the punishment handed out to Arthur and George?"

"Arthur deserves what he got but I do feel a bit sorry for George. He had retired from cloud work. It was Arthur that persuaded him to help with the theft."

Conversation then turned to the question of who aided them at Wythenshawe.

"It didn't take long to track that one down. At the time of the theft there were only four people on duty and three of them were together. When I crossed-examined Ronnie Green he admitted his part in it all."

Mr Spite then went on to say that he had sacked Ronnie on the spot, not just for aiding a theft but also for endangering a passenger flight from New York. The Civil Aviation Authority was still considering bringing a case against all those involved with endangering Flight NY2U from New York.

As far as Larry Oliver and Oscar Blowhard were concerned, it was a great relief to have the Drip back. Once it had been checked out by the engineers at Black, Black & Blackemore's they could get back into weather making on demand. It was somewhat ironic that their first job was delivering a mist just off the Isle-of-Wight as part of a sailing skills competition, but at least they didn't get charged for it. In fact, they got paid for it. All this just goes to prove that you can't steal a mist without eventually being seen through!

TWO DROPS DON'T MAKE A DRIZZLE

2013 will long be remembered as the summer Britain has waited for, for many years. To see the sun is special but to see it on several consecutive days is very special. Long neglected skills come back in a spell of nice weather. The silence of a summer Sunday is broken by the sound of a million mowers all busy at work, along with the chorus of hedge-cutters. The sound of house and car alarms gets drowned out by the rush to tidy neglected lawns but there is still no getting away from the daily cavalcade of sirens care of the Police, Ambulance and Fire Service going about their routine business.

The old habit of sitting out in the yard and reading a newspaper to induce sleep is rekindled in a good summer, but the art of knotting handkerchiefs to create a sun protecting form of headwear is on the wane. Good summers equal barbecues and the smells waft across the neighbourhood. Portable radios are shared by households but not always appreciated by all. Good summers mean good sales for sun lotion, and natural tans replace those provided by sun beds. Girls get more attractive and young men get more frisky.

The holiday business thrives when the sun is out and blue skies are accompanied by long convoys of cars to well established resorts by the sea where you can buy the same stuff you bought last year and the year before. Staple diets of pie and chips is just as good in the sun as it is in the rain and there is no shortage of places offering it up for consumption. Parking spots rapidly fill and late arrivals have a tough time, especially when kids are on board. Kids hate travelling in hot cars going round in circles in full view of golden sand and an inviting sea.

2013 was turning into a brilliant year for those involved with the holiday trade. From one end of the country to the other, everyone involved with the business was saying how good things were after years of abysmal weather. There is no doubt that Great Britain has a lot to offer the holidaymaker and when combined with good weather there is no place better to be, or least that's what places like Blackpool and Scarborough said on their publicity leaflets.

The current financial climate and the increased cost of holidays abroad were combining to make holidaying at home in the UK more attractive, and the good weather helped considerably. Many overseas destinations were off-limits for a lot of folk due to the turmoil going on there and places like Torquay and Great Yarmouth were back in vogue. The girls on the beach look just as good in Filey as they do in Benidorm and there are no euros involved.

The British economy was getting a boost as holidaymakers spent at home rather than abroad, reducing the Nation's trade deficit into the bargain. Yes, 2013 was turning into a memorable year in more ways than one.

Brits and the Sun

Rain and wind are weather ingredients that make British people what they are. Wind and rain are ingrained in British culture and although many like to escape to sunnier climes now and again, they are always drawn back to what they are comfortable with. Sun is nice but often it makes life restricted. There is nothing like rain and wind to make people want to get on with some kind of work and anyway, what can you do with a tan other than watch it go away. You can have too much of the sun and when you do, it gets you down and that's exactly what a lot of holidaymakers were feeling in Scarborough this summer.

After hours of sunshine, nothing had that nice fresh feeling about it and prim flowers in flower beds were wilting in the heat. Unpleasant smells increased in intensity and pesky flies seemed to multiply under the midday sun. Scarborough's visitors were doing what they could to hide from the rays that had travelled billions of miles to hit them. Large umbrellas appeared in hundreds on the beach and those who had not staked a claim there sat in park shelters, bus shelters and under any other cover they could find, all clear evidence of the craving by the British for wind and rain. Every café, pub and other watering hole was full of humanity trying to evade those pervasive rays.

It is only fair to point out that not everybody objected to the sun. Young women on the beach invited the rays by exposing as much of their flesh as they legally dare in order to change colour, and young men adored them for it although the change of colour was less important to them. Flesh and curves were higher up the enticing scales for these hot-blooded males. A new phenomenon one could now witness on the beaches, and elsewhere for that matter, was the number of young men and women who had their heads buried in an iPod or mobile phone or some other technological gadgetry as if they had a desire to disconnect with the here and now. To the casual observer it seemed as if there was another world out there that they had not made contact with, although overhearing any conversations between mobile users did not inspire one to think that if there is another world out there that it was much of a place for intellect.

"What are you doing now John?"

"Nothing much. Just on my computer at home. What about you?"

"Same really. Just getting a tan but it's boring."

One could detect a growing lethargy with all this sun at Scarborough and folk were becoming a bit tetchy. The kids were becoming a nuisance and one or two dogs sniffing around rubbish receptacles became victims of rocket-propelled right feet which would not have disgraced a Championship League football match.

If the sun kept shining there was going to be trouble in Scarborough and there were not enough pubs to quell it. The Town Council had a meeting to debate it and see what could be done to cool things down. The chairman of the Council, Fred Arbuthnot, was the first to speak.

"We need to find a way to freshen things up."

"Them young folks are fresh enough as it is judging by what they get up to on the beach."

"Nevertheless councilor, I think we need to cool things down."

"Now that's something I agree with," replied one of the attendees.

A spirited debate then occurred on what was needed to cool down holidaymakers suffering from too much sun. In the end it was the obvious that won the day – rain. Plain old fashioned rain was needed. Not in large quantities, just enough to give an invigorating outdoor shower feeling which could also bring new life to all those flowers the council had planted, and dampen down the unpleasant aromas permeating the places that wouldn't normally smell.

The council had a two and half hour recess after reaching such a mind-boggling decision. There was no point in rushing into an agreement and a few pints might provide some inspiration. Returning to the council chamber after a few pints was easier said than done as was plain to see when only a half of the council made it back.

As is custom, the chairman started the proceedings.

"I shtink, sorry, I think."

"You got it right first time mate!"

When the guffaws decreased, (they don't laugh in council meetings or government meetings, they always guffaw. It's posher.) the chairman started again.

"What we have agreed, fellow councillors is to rain."

A huge clap of appreciation followed which also followed a custom that goes back several hundred years except that they were different councillors then.

"I suggest we want light rain, more of a dribble than a heavy drop."

"You mean drizzle, not dribble, you daft bugger."

"Order, order!"

"Two pints of best bitter please."

Things were beginning to deteriorate and it took the town clerk and a couple of beefy council workers to calm things. Evidently, the sun affects councilors as well as holidaymakers.

"Well there we have it, we need drizzle but the question is when and where from."

The *where from* was not a difficult question to answer. Scarborough had had dealings with Wythenshawe Weather Centre in connection with the making of an episode for a TV detective series. A drizzle could be ordered from there and it would be cheaper than rain.

The question of *when* received longer debate, which continued, until no-one in the chamber remained awake. It was going to be down to the clerk of the council to make the necessary arrangements.

From Hacking to Fracking

Puffy was standing outside the lounge door of the Slaidburn home he shared with his Captain. He was waiting for an opportune moment to take in a morning coffee and biscuit but that moment had not yet presented itself. He had left his Captain earlier with a copy of the Daily Gloom and, judging by the ranting and raving he had heard, there was something in it that he did not agree with. Not that that was anything unusual these days, for his Captain was displeased with many things connected with the governance of his beloved country and he held the politicians of the day responsible. The point was, though, that if Puffy mistimed his entry he was sure to feel the full ferocity of his Captain's feelings. In spite of that, it was the temperature of the coffee that would ultimately determine the time of his appearance; he could not let it go cold. The ranting had subsided and, taking a deep breath, Puffy knocked to announce his arrival and then arrived, tray and coffee in hand.

"Dam protesters! Why doesn't the Government get a grip?" asked the Captain.

A short silence fell as Puffy placed the tray on the coffee table in front of the Captain's favourite chair.

"You know, these engineers have found enough gas under the country to supply us with all we need for the next twenty to thirty years. Just think of it! We would be completely independent in terms of gas for all that time. The country would not have to pay what another country chooses to demand from us and the supply would be guaranteed and not subject to the political whims of a bunch of foreign political wafflers."

Puffy nodded in agreement and stood his ground. Experience had taught him that his best move would be to let his Captain burn his emotions out before stampeding for the door.

"They reckon that this gas find is the biggest thing since the discovery of North Sea oil and yet they are protesting about getting it from under the ground."

It might be a good idea to appear interested thought Puffy, who then made a contribution to the subject.

"I suppose you are referring to this business of fracking, skipper?"

"Too damn right I am! From hacking to fracking, there's always something these days. Getting this gas out would be nothing compared with what had to be done to get coal and just think where the country would be if we hadn't done that."

"I hadn't thought about that," said Puffy.

"Fracking could also provide employment for many people which in our present state would not be a bad thing."

At this juncture, Puffy made a fateful mistake that would delay his departure considerably and he would end up kicking himself.

"That's fine providing those being employed are our own people."

"That's another damn issue these political bods can't get a grip of. The country is going to the dogs and fast."

It was essential for Puffy to redeem the situation in some way or another and he had a stab at it.

"Mind you, skipper, sometimes going further afield for your labour is not such a bad thing. Look at that lovely thing behind the bar in the Hark to Bounty. She comes from France and what a beauty she is. The landlord says his takings have gone up in quantum leaps since she started pulling pints."

"Yeah, and the hem on her skirt has gone up too since she came on the scene."

"Oh, you have noticed then?"

Cirrus Cumulus was momentarily thrown off his fracking and whilst he paused to enjoy the images flooding into his laboured mind, Puffy made good his escape.

The phone rang and Puffy answered. It was Goldilocks on the other end and she had details of a job that he and Cirrus might be interested in.

"Skipper, its Mr Spite's secretary on the line with information about a job."

Cirrus turned his thoughts from the hemline of one attractive female to that of another.

"Hello, Goldilocks, what can I do for you?"

After the chuckle at the other end had died down, Goldilocks got on with a description of a job in Scarborough.

Scarborough Drizzle

On arrival at Wythenshawe, Cirrus and his flight engineer, Puffy, set about checking that their cloud machine, *the Nimbus,* was free from any defects and suitably provisioned for the job in hand over Scarborough. Satisfied that everything was in order, the two crew members cast their eyes over the weather plan.

The *Nimbus* in cloud form would stand offshore from Scarborough during the day but would fly the short distance to the resort in order to cover it in shadow from 7-00pm onwards. A light drizzle had been ordered between 8-00pm and 9-00pm followed by their departure to loiter again offshore. The Town Council had ordered drizzle for Monday, Wednesday and Friday evening which meant that there would be a lot of loitering to do, but that didn't make this job any different from a hundred others that the *Nimbus* had been involved with.

Cirrus and Puffy kept themselves busy on board the *Nimbus*, reading whilst waiting for darkness to fall. When it did fall, Cirrus started up the four fan duct motors and checked that they were running smoothly before he opened the throttles to taxi forward out of its usual parking spot inside Wythenshawe's cavernous hangar. Turning the *Nimbus* to face the hangar doors, the hangar lights started to dim and had completely extinguished by the time the huge doors had opened to reveal a black world outside.

The *Nimbus* was brought to a stop on the large concrete apron outside the hangar doors and Puffy contacted Wythenshawe's control centre for clearance to ascend into the night sky. With clearance given, the *Nimbus* lifted off mother earth and rapidly ascended into the darkness. This was always a thrilling experience and this occasion was no less so as the cloud machine climbed to 5,000 feet before hovering. Cirrus activated the Identification Beacon before heading off to the Irish Sea. The ID beacon enabled any radar on the ground or in an aircraft, or indeed in any other cloud machine, to identify the blip that would represent the *Nimbus* on their radar displays.

At 5,000 feet the *Nimbus* headed west to a position over the Irish Sea offshore from Liverpool. Although nature's cloud creations were heading east on a westerly wind, no-one down below could witness the strange scene above because of the darkness. At the appropriate position, Cirrus brought the *Nimbus* to a hover and Puffy began his part in the job. Some 3,000,000 gallons of the Irish Sea were atomised and a Cumberland Grey cloud began to embrace the *Nimbus*. Once the cloud had reached a size that met with the approval of Puffy, he continued atomising but used the sea to fill the saddle tanks fitted on the outside of the *Nimbus* and when they were full he turned further supplies coming aboard into ice in the machine's storage refrigerators.

Once loaded, the *Nimbus* joined nature's convoys heading east in the night sky and its crew could be confident that they would be anonymous to anyone peering into the night. Only radar controllers would be aware of the night flight by the Nimbus but even they would not be able to pick it out with the mark one eyeball amongst nature's puffy sky creatures.

The Sunday night flight across the Pennines to Yorkshire did not take long and the Yorkshire coastline appeared on the TV console on the flight-deck in a relatively short time. Peering at his Plan Position Indicator (PPI), Cirrus could see that he had been flying on the correct heading; Scarborough was just ahead. It was still dark but the moon, shining through the gaps in the cloud convoy, was illuminating both of Scarborough's bays and the harbour stood out particularly well. Very soon it would be time to bring the *Nimbus* to a hover again and let nature's convoy carry on. Once in the hover the crew could get some sleep. It would be almost twelve hours before they would be required to deliver drizzle and, until then, sleep was a nice option.

As Scarborough's early risers took a morning stroll along the promenade there wasn't the slightest inkling that the offshore Cumberland Grey, stationary in the sky, was there to perform a job on behalf of the Town Council. To be fair, it was a bit difficult to pick out amongst the busy movement of other clouds heading across the North Sea for the Netherlands.

One man in Scarborough was, however, taking a particular interest in the morning sky and that was Chairman of the Town Council, Fred

Arbuthnot. Fred was anxious that the Council plan was going to work. It cost a lot of money to hire a drizzle and he wanted value or drizzle for money. He had supported the plan and, consequently, he did not want to get egg on his face. Drizzle would be fine but not egg! Scour the morning sky as he might, Fred could not pick anything out that might be what would be delivering Scarborough's refreshing and invigorating evening drizzle. The wind- propelled clouds drifting overhead and into the distance all looked rather similar. Perhaps Scarborough's delivery had not arrived yet.

By mid-morning, holidaymakers thronged the beach and promenade and in spite of tempers that began to fray with the continuous sunshine. The oppressive atmosphere was proving too much for some. There was a limit to how much ice-cream anyone could take and tea with sand in it wasn't much help.

"What we want, Gladys, is a good shower of rain to freshen things up," said Bert, on holiday from Batley.

Gladys couldn't agree more at this moment in time as she attempted to spread a watery tub of butter on a sandwich for the kids.

Bikini-clad young women tiptoed into the North Sea before dashing out again. The North Sea always seemed to be insulated from the heat of the sun, no matter what time of the year. Children tend to be made of sterner stuff than bikini-clad young women, and a steady stream of industrious types made hundreds of journeys, armed with buckets and spades, to bring back to fledgling new sand-castles quantities of that North Sea liquid to fill moats. The disappearance of the liquid into the moat sand did not seem to dent their enthusiasm and it helped occasionally to empty a bucket or two onto Dad or a bikini-clad elder sister.

Fred could detect, as the day went on, that folk were getting irritable with all this sunshine. He was a man of the world and appreciated the role of rain in an Englishman's life. Englishmen are brought up to know that you can have too much of a good thing. Rain gives people a break and something to talk about and the British are renowned around the world for talking about the weather. Rain is an essential ingredient for weather variety. People from countries like France, Italy and Spain don't understand why the British are at home with rain, but Fred Arbuthnot did and hoped he would soon see some at Scarborough.

On board the *Nimbus*, Cirrus and Puffy had just enjoyed a salad for tea and the time was approaching for delivery of Scarborough's drizzle. Getting into his pilot's seat, Cirrus opened the throttles and the four fan duct motors propelled the craft forward into the prevailing westerly wind. The *Nimbus* edged forward towards the coast travelling through one or two of nature's creatures at the same time but no-one in Scarborough took any notice save Fred Arbuthnot, who was still concerned about egg.

At 7-00pm the Cumberland Grey, care of the *Nimbus,* sat above the resort at 5,000 feet. This was the position that it would drizzle from but for the moment it just cast a cooling shadow over the place, much to the holidaymakers' relief. It was also to the relief of the Council Chairman who had been following the track of the cloud since it first moved in the opposite direction to all the others.

At 7-30pm the *Nimbus* descended to 2,500 feet and its shadow brought suspicions to those looking skywards that something was about to happen. The heat of the day had not dissipated and strained nerves got the better of several folks who had sought relief in the town's pubs. The local Police Force had several call outs and was busy trying to quell several fights. It could only get worse as the evening drew on and Fred Arbuthnot kept looking at his watch as he counted down the time to drizzle.

At 7-45pm the *Nimbus* descended to 1,000 feet, its intended drizzle height, and Scarborough got darker. The heat trapped between the Cumberland Grey and the surface of the earth on which the resort had been built got even more oppressive and several more Police sirens could be heard as the local force sped to the scene of new fights and disputes.

As 8-00pm approached, those standing close to Fred could hear him murmuring to himself as he looked at his watch.

"Come on, come on, drizzle for God's sake or at least for Scarborough," he could be heard saying.

8-00pm arrived and a full five minutes passed but there was no drizzle. A further ten minutes passed but all that Fred had felt was two solitary drops of rain.

On board the *Nimbus*, Puffy had set all the controls on his panel for drizzle and right now he was sitting with his feet up on the chart table observing the instruments that were his responsibility. This was an easy job that would end at 9-00pm, at which time they would head back out offshore and wait for Wednesday. It was something of a mistake that Puffy indulged himself reading a book rather than watch the instruments that would tell him what was happening. *"Drizzling on Scarborough, what a lark,"* thought Puffy.

After thirty minutes standing under a dark cloud in an oppressive heat, Fred was literally steaming. He had felt two solitary drops of rain. Fred was of the opinion that two drops of rain don't make a drizzle and if this was the best the people at Wythenshawe Weather Centre could come up or perhaps that should be down with then it wasn't good enough. The next thirty minutes brought no drizzle, only an uncomfortable climate that Scarborough could well do without.

At 9-00pm the cloud above moved out towards the sea and took with it the shadow that had hidden the oncoming of a sunset. The temperature fell as did several individuals hell bent on settling some dispute with the aid of knuckles, but the local Police Force soon had them in care. It was somewhat ironic that fighting pairs ended up sharing a cell for the night but that was the way of it. The Town Council chairman was most unimpressed and the egg on his face forced him into action.

"It's Spite here. What can I do for you at this late hour, Mr Arbuthnot?"

I'll tell you what you can do for me. Bring me some bloody drizzle!"

Mr Spite, the Superintendent at Wythenshawe Weather Centre, had not been expecting this kind of a call and replied by trying to placate the Council chairman.

"I dispatched one of my most trusted cloud machine owners. Something must have gone amiss."

"Something went amiss all right, it was a damn drizzle that went amiss." Mr Arbuthnot continued, *"I stood on the promenade for an hour and all I felt in that time was two solitary drops of rain. Now in my book, two drops of rain don't make a drizzle and I want to know what you are going to do about it?"*

Clearly, without making enquiries, there was nothing that Mr Spite could do and he had to endure a long Yorkshire haranguing before he could put the phone down. What was obvious was that he needed to speak to the crew of the *Nimbus* urgently to establish what was going on.

A Problem Tracked Down

"What do you mean, we didn't drizzle?" replied the Captain of the *Nimbus* in response to a call from Wythenshawe's Superintendent.

"At exactly 8-00pm we drizzled on Scarborough for a solid hour," went on Cirrus.

"Well you must have been in the wrong place or something went wrong."

Cirrus felt a little indignant that Mr Spite would seriously suggest he had drizzled on the wrong place and told him so.

"Well if you were in the right place, something must have gone wrong. Check your instruments and see if they give you a clue."

Cirrus asked Puffy to take a look at the gauges that give an indication of the water in the craft's saddle tanks and the ice stored in the onboard refrigerators. If the *Nimbus* had drizzled, then its Cumberland Grey would have started to get smaller but it would have been automatically topped up by making vapour from the contents of both the saddle tanks and refrigerators.

"Well blow me down skipper. The saddle tanks and refrigerators are all still full!"

When this information was relayed back to Mr Spite there was nothing for it but to return to Wythenshawe and let the engineers from Black, Black

& Blackemore's take a look. The unfortunate part about this was that the Town Council chairman would have to be informed and the prospect of doing that was not something that was to be looked forward to.

Drizzling on Scarborough was put back by a week and the Council got a large reduction in the fee it had to pay. Meanwhile the *Nimbus* headed back to the Irish Sea where it rained heavily to get rid of its cloud. In the darkness of the early hours of Wednesday morning it made its naked way to Wythenshawe where, having gained clearance, it descended to land on the concrete apron outside the huge hangar that housed all the cloud machines. The hangar doors were already open and the *Nimbus* taxied in to its usual parking slot and as it did so the doors closed and the hangar lights came on.

Engineers from Black, Black & Blackemore's were already waiting to get on-board as Cirrus and Puffy opened the craft's door and deployed the access ladder. Mr Spite was anxious to get the *Nimbus* drizzling on Scarborough as fast as he could. It was essential to minimise the loss that this job was now going to incur. The crew was a little disappointed that they couldn't leave the Centre for a few hours whilst the fault was detected but Puffy took full advantage by dashing along to Mr Spite's secretary's office, where a certain lady that he called Goldilocks would be pleased to see him.

Puffy looked at the title on the door; it read *Secretary to the Superintendent – Miss Joanne Black.* It looked very official and he knocked and waited.

"Come in."

With that invitation, Puffy entered and his breath was taken away by the sight of blonde-haired Joanne sitting behind a forbidding looking desk. It was a mystery to him why she was nicknamed Goldilocks but he could live with it.

"You're a sight for sore eyes, Goldilocks. How do you keep looking so good?"

Miss Black chuckled at the compliment before replying.

31

"Hark at you Percival White. You should be drizzling on Scarborough. How come you are here?"

"I've swopped drizzling for drooling and anyway, what sort of a greeting is that? Aren't you pleased to see me?"

Smiling, Joanne got up out of her chair and her tallness and slim figure became the focus of Puffy's attention. She was taller than Puffy but in a wrestling configuration that was of little consequence.

Moving gracefully from behind her desk, Joanne came into full view and the addition of legs melted her admirer. The office settee looked most inviting but there was some serious snogging to be done before moving on to more advanced stuff. She not only looked good but she also tasted good and smelled good. What's more, she felt fantastic and the settee was taking on more of an importance. Detecting Puffy's amorous intentions, Joanne felt it appropriate to point out that it was a risky business being frisky in the Superintendent's secretary's office. He could come barging in at any time. Puffy was a little disappointed but had to agree that she had a point. As a matter of fact she had several points, all of which he had a desire to explore, but for the moment he would have to settle for the current hold he had on her which actually felt pretty good. The settee would have to wait for a more opportune time, but something was salvaged out of the situation as the pair embraced each other for another round of stand-up snogging accompanied by a multitude of arm movements, mostly initiated by Puffy.

"When this job is over you must come and stay at my place in Slaidburn," said Puffy as he came up for air.

"That would be lovely," replied Goldilocks between short breaths.

This wonderful session of erotic greeting had to end and it did so as Mr Spite burst into the office. At first he was a little taken aback by what he saw but he rapidly got a grip of himself and announced – *"White, you better get back to the Nimbus. The craft's been fixed. Go and find your Captain and get on your way."*

Puffy could clearly see that the Superintendent was not pleased with what he had barged into and, feeling rather meek in the circumstances, he dropped everything, which in this case was Goldilocks, and left the office to find his skipper.

Looking at his secretary, Mr Spite said, rather sternly, *"I wish you would leave your love life for somewhere more private in future and, anyway, don't you think Percival White is a little old for you?"*

Looking straight into Mr Spite's eyes, she replied in a seductive voice, *"I prefer men of the world; they bring so much more to a relationship."*

The Superintendent coughed and spluttered and rushed into his own office, nearly tripping over the corner of the carpet as he made his escape.

Back to Drizzling

By Wednesday evening the engineers from Black, Black & Blackemore's had repaired the fault on the *Nimbus,* which turned out to be one of the many black boxes which housed some electronic gadgetry, in this case, drizzling gadgetry. As soon as it was dark, the *Nimbus* ascended into the night sky in its usual fashion and then headed for the Irish Sea in order to create a Cumberland Grey cloud and to store water and ice. Having recreated its Scarborough package, the journey to the east coast was embarked on alongside nature's creations.

By midday on Thursday the *Nimbus* was back in its hovering location offshore from its seaside destination and Fred Arbuthnot was most pleased with the speed at which Wythenshawe had resolved the problem. He was equally pleased that this evening, along with the next, he would get the drizzle he and a few thousand holidaymakers were desperate for. A hot, dry Scarborough was not as idyllic as some may think. Wilted flowers were a poor substitute for the colourful blossoms that had originally been planted and there was a general feeling of exhaustion about the place except for the young men eyeing up the young bikini-clad women tiptoeing on the edge of the waterline. Even the seagulls seemed lethargic. Drizzle was going to be welcome.

At 7-00pm Fred spotted a cloud heading inland from offshore and he continued to observe it for thirty minutes until it was overhead. The shadow it cast upon the ground was reassuring to a point but, of course, it had been here before. As the time progressed towards 8-00pm it got darker and darker. There was a general feeling that something was about to happen and word spread rapidly. Both the locals and those on holiday came out to stand in the shadow of the big grey cloud above and wait. Fred started to count down as 8-00pm approached and he felt the drizzle on his arm spot on time as did thousands of others, and a huge cheer rang out across the resort. A few minutes of drizzle was sheer ecstasy after weeks of dry weather. Almost instantaneously the mood changed. People felt refreshed and jumped for drizzle as they celebrated what they thought nature had delivered, but Fred Arbuthnot and the Town Council knew better. It was a strange sight to see folk looking up at the grey cloud whilst it drizzled on them and they laughed whilst it did. Fights broke up as sozzled contestants took to the drizzle as an alternative.

The egg on Fred's face was washed away and his fellow Councillors had nothing but admiration for his drizzling prowess. By 9-00pm it was all over until it was repeated on the morrow, but it had been a great success. The whole of Scarborough and its inhabitants, permanent and temporary, had been invigorated, not to mention the flora and the fauna. There was dancing in the street and celebrations took place on every street corner.

Those visitors from overseas were well aware of the British obsession with weather but never in their wildest dreams did it occur to them how serious it was taken. To have such a strong desire for it to rain seemed slightly insane to them but here they were in Scarborough witnessing the celebration of drizzling! There was really no accounting for the mind-set of the British and it would be something to tell folks when they got back home. It appeared that the ultimate in holiday happiness was getting drizzled on.

By 9-00pm on Friday night the job was complete and the *Nimbus*, with its greatly diminished Cumberland Grey, could make its way back across the Pennines to the Irish Sea. The wind had dropped and hence, with a bit of luck, the crew could dump the remains of its cloud offshore from

Liverpool and get back to Wythenshawe before dawn broke. It would be nice to get home for a few hours, they thought.

The forecast had changed. It was unlikely that Scarborough would want the *Nimbus* back again. There would, therefore, be a chance for a longer stay in Slaidburn before another job was undertaken. Puffy was quick to react to this news.

"Skipper, would you mind if I invited Goldilocks over to our place for a few days when we get back?"

Cirrus couldn't help smiling to himself. It had never occurred to him that his Flight Engineer and Mr Spite's secretary would ever have struck up a romantic relationship.

Nevertheless, he was happy that his colleague had found romance.

"Not at all Puffy. She will be a refreshing change from drizzling!"

Not everyone in Scarborough might agree!

A DIP INTO THE PAST

"*T*hese windfarms are getting too numerous,*" thought Cirrus as he read about the next lot of developments in the Daily Gloom over his morning coffee in his Slaidburn home.

"If they were all out at sea it wouldn't be too bad but on land they are getting too numerous and they don't add anything to the scenery. When there were only a few there was a novelty value about them, but now!"

The abundance of windfarms made Cirrus draw a parallel with uncontrolled immigration and it didn't do much for his digestive system, but his thoughts were interrupted as his faithful engineer, Puffy, entered the room.

"You know, Puffy, all these windfarms only produce a small amount of the electricity that the country needs. There is no escape from the need to build new power stations.

We can't rely on wind and sun. I've just read about a solar farm that is going to be established. Can you imagine what it is going to look like when the country is covered by wind and solar farms?"

Puffy knew from experience that it was best to agree with his skipper when he had a bee in his bonnet.

"Where are they going to grow chips is what I want to know skipper?"

Cirrus looked up at his engineer in disbelief but left it at that, but Puffy had more to say.

"They may have nowhere left to grow anything but the landowners will still get rich."

"That's very perceptive of you Puffy. The problem with this country is that it's full of objectors. Every time the Government wants to get started on building a power station there is opposition of some sort. That reminds me, we better start stocking up on candles."

Puffy picked up the crockery that needed washing and was just about to head to the kitchen when Cirrus began again.

"I fancy doing something different."

Puffys ear's pricked up and he earnestly waited to hear what was meant by different.

"For a long time I've thought about visiting the Cloud Museum in deeper Salford but never got round to it."

This brought about memories of a conversation the two intrepid weather-makers had had with some of their retired colleagues in the *Head in the Sky* rest home in Grange-over-Sands. Whilst the Museum had been open for a few years now, the crew of the *Nimbus* had never got round to making a visit, but that was about to change.

"I think we'll go and take a look, Puffy. Take a look at the computer and see if you can find out when it's open will you?"

When Puffy had done that, it was agreed that they would go the following day.

The Cloud Museum was situated on Pacific Way in deeper Salford, adjacent to Black, Black & Blackemore's factory on the banks of the Manchester Ship Canal. The building was large but rather nondescript since it had no architectural merit. There was only a small sign over the entrance to announce it was the Cloud Museum and the curator's name was Dr William Overcast.

They entered the Museum and realised that they had not brought with them their *Guild of Cloud Owners* membership cards which would have given them free access.

The entry fee was not exorbitant and it included the free use of the toilets. On either side of the entry corridor, which accommodated the pay desk, was a café and a souvenir shop but it was the main hall that lay ahead that looked most enticing. From the position of the pay desk they caught a glimpse of several cloud machines, and they couldn't wait to get inside and take a good look.

Armed with a Museum brochure, Cirrus and Puffy stepped into the main hall and were overtaken by a sense of awe at all that was on view. Two cloud machines hung from the ceiling and two others were on view at ground level accompanied by a number of mock-ups showing various stages of development. Along each side of the main hall there were three rooms and, consulting their brochures, they decided to view them first.

RAF Cloud Corps

The first room that the crew of the *Nimbus* visited told the story of cloud machines in military service.

The RAF Cloud Corps had been formed in 1942 with its headquarters and training establishment initially based in the famous airship hangars at Cardington in Bedfordshire. Crew training was carried out here and all of the RAF's fleet of cloud machines was housed in the cavernous hangars. Trained aircrew could be recognised by the emblem of a small cloud above the wings on the left hand side of their uniforms.

In 1943 a new training centre was established at Wythenshawe with its own huge hangar and the RAF Cloud Corps transferred its activities to this tailor-made facility.

During the Second World War, RAF cloud machines had largely been used to assist the Atlantic convoys, deterring German submarines and helping to discover the launch sites of the German V1 weapons along the coast of

Belgium and France. There were stories of cloud machines being used to provide showers for Allied troops, particularly in the deserts of Egypt and Tunisia, but no-one got a medal for it.

The RAF Cloud Corps was somewhat short-lived and it disbanded in 1946 after just four years of existence, and in 1947 a memorial plaque was erected in the former training establishment in Wythenshawe which had inscribed on it the names of those killed on active cloud service. Looking at a photo of the plaque, Cirrus spotted the name of Sgt J.Windfall RAF. Cirrus remembered Jimmy Windfall from a conversation he had had with some of the retired chaps at the rest home in Grange-over-Sands.

"So that's who they were talking about," remarked Cirrus.

Photographs, maps and other memorabilia were scattered around the room and both Cirrus and Puffy were reluctant to leave, but there was a lot more to see.

The room had rekindled memories of a great day visiting the *Head in the Sky* rest home and listening to old-timers, Alf Fisher and his pals George and Fred as they reminisced about their time in the Cloud Corps. This place had made it all real.

Cloud Machine Manufacture

The second room into which Cirrus and Puffy went told the story of the world's only cloud machine manufacturer and one of Salford's claims to fame. The story began in 1940 when aircraft designer Douglas Black and his brother, aeronautical engineer William Black, met up with weather scientist Frank Blackemore. The three of them agreed to construct a machine that could create a cloud.

The idea had originated from a need to know what the country's wartime enemy was doing without being spotted. If a flying machine could be created that could create and immerse itself in cloud, it could spy from the sky with impunity.

Douglas and William Black would create the machine whilst Frank Blackemore would pioneer the making of a cloud. The establishment of Black, Black & Blackemore's in deeper Salford took place on May 5th, 1940.

Frank designed a piece of equipment which he called an atomiser. The atomiser produced a beam of energy, rather like a laser beam, which when impacting with water evaporated it. The vapour then travelled up to the energy source and gathered around it in the form of a cloud which was grey and voluminous. Frank came from Cumberland and hence he called them Cumberland Greys. He recognised at an early stage of development that the best results were yielded by using water from particular sources.

The atomiser was installed on the underside of the first flying machine designed and built by the Black Brothers. This first machine looked like an autogiro, with an engine in the nose that drove a propeller and a rotor on top of the airframe. The aircraft flew well but when the first attempts at creating a cloud were conducted they ran into their first problem. The cloud completely covered the aircraft and they couldn't see where they were going or, more importantly, they couldn't see what the enemy was doing. This first problem was overcome after much trial and error by relocating the atomiser to the rear underside of the airframe. It was found that by doing this the cloud that they created was kept to the rear when it started to form and the airflow from the propeller kept it there providing it was not rotating too fast. The only drawback with this arrangement was that the cloud could not hover and the nose of the craft stuck out from it, but from a height of a few thousand feet it was not really noticeable.

In 1941 the Government began taking an interest in the pioneering cloud work of Black, Black & Blackemore's but had some doubts given the problems associated with getting rid of the cloud after use. Frank turned his scientific mind to cloud disposal and found his answer in nature's work. He designed a simple condenser which, when installed aboard the cloud-making aircraft, sucked the cloud vapour in through holes placed around the airframe, condensed it, and forced it out as rain through more holes on the underside. This clinched the idea as far as the Government was concerned. *"Go spy as a cloud, rain, and come home."* What a crafty way of doing things!

The RAF Cloud Corps was formed in 1942 and the business set up by the Black Brothers and Frank Blackemore was now on a firm footing. Business boomed in the war years but when it ended in 1945 and the RAF Cloud Corps disbanded in 1946, the future looked bleak. It was most fortunate that the Meteorological Office had been taking an interest in the work being done in Salford and felt that research ought to continue into weather-making, for they could see some potential in it.

The Meteorological Office took over the former RAF Cloud Corps centre at Wythenshawe in 1946 and gave it its current title, *Wythenshawe Weather Centre.* For the next four years it conducted weather-making research using the ex RAF machines and ex RAF crews. Black, Black & Blackemore's provided engineering support during these years and the firm just managed to survive these lean times.

In the early 1950s the Meteorological Office relinquished its interest in the weather- making centre and sold it off to an organisation that would go on to offer weather by order provided by modern machines owned privately but chartered by the centre. This was really the beginning of the present day arrangements.

Cloud manufacture went from strength to strength in Salford over the next seventy years and still continues to do so. Great strides have been made in technology and what cloud machines can do. The various developments were on view in the large hall. Each time new developments had been installed on their machines, the manufacturer had highlighted them by allocating a grading system to each new model. The original was graded one star, the next two star and so on.

The sons and daughters of the original founders continue to have a keen interest in the company. Douglas Black's son, Johnny, is the current company's test pilot whilst William Black's daughter, Sheila, is on the Board of Directors at the newly established Weather Making Research Centre at Llanbedr. Sheila is married to Professor W Flood, Head of the

Research Centre. Ronnie Blackemore, son of founder, Frank, is the current company flight test engineer.

Whilst Black, Black & Blackemore's have been the sole manufacturer of cloud machines, their sales have been confined to the owners chartered by Wythenshawe Weather Centre and they are relatively few in numbers. Development work, and after sales service, which is very extensive, have kept the firm going. Exports would have been helpful in financial terms but the Government had prevented that without giving any explanation as to why. At least the UK has a monopoly when it comes to making weather to order and it can deliver anywhere in the world.

The manufacturing side of things could never have survived if it was not for the development of a workable infrastructure and that's what Cirrus and Puffy decided they would take a look at next, but first they would call in the cafeteria and have a coffee.

"I never dreamed this place would be so interesting, skipper," remarked Puffy.

"Neither did I but it tells our history very well and we have only seen a small part of it so far."

The crew of the Nimbus sat drinking coffee whilst browsing through the brochures they had purchased and little was said between them. They were simply enthralled by what they were learning about the line of business that earned them both a living.

Developing Infrastructure

Cirrus and Puffy entered the third room off the main hall to learn about the infrastructure that had emerged to manage weather-making and delivery. In the early 1950's the Meteorological Office relinquished control of Wythenshawe Weather Centre and its management passed to a group of cloud machine crews that had purchased their own weather-making craft and formed the 'Guild of Cloud Owners'. The Guild had the responsibility of running the Centre and looking after the interests of the owners. One of the first tasks performed by the Guild was the production of a publication titled – *The Cloud Machine Operators Rules of Operation Manual.* This manual standardised the way everybody in the weather-making business worked. This was rapidly followed by the development of a *Compendium of water by grades* which was intended to assist crews when it came to making clouds to a particular standard, although it has to be said that, these days, technology almost allows any quality of cloud to be manufactured from any quality of water, but the compendium was a valuable start.

After a few years of operation, the *Guild* began printing a monthly newsletter called *The Monthly Downpour* which was intended to keep all the cloud machine owners aware of what was happening in the world of weather, and it proved to be most popular.

In the early years of its existence, the *Guild* became acutely aware of the fact that now that the RAF Cloud Corps had disbanded there were no facilities in existence to train new crews and, further to this, current crews were grossly deficient in a number of important skills. In order to deal with these matters a *Training Centre* was opened on a disused airfield at Bishops Court in County Down, Northern Ireland. At the culmination of training, licences were issued to successful pilots and flight engineers. There was some resistance initially by current crews to allow themselves to be subjected to a training regime, but in time everyone did and standards improved enormously. *Bishops Court Training Centre* courses were now eagerly sought after for they were also an opportunity to meet up with long-time no-see colleagues. An example of a cloud machine pilot's licence hung on the wall and it was that of the late *Al Blighty.*

In the 1960s the *Guild* made great strides forward in the area of insurance for cloud machine owners and comprehensive cover became available for the first time. Premiums were, however, subject to applicants having a clean licence. Anyone with an endorsement for infringing the rules of operation would pay more, but there was the benefit that if an owner made no claim for compensation over a period of time, then the premium would be reduced. In other words, there was a no-claim bonus.

At the same time that the *Guild* was negotiating an insurance deal it was also looking at the general condition of the cloud machines its members owned, and it was not impressed. There was a fair amount of dedicated neglect on show amongst the weather-making fraternity and it was felt that this would make insurance negotiations difficult. When all is said and done, who would want to insure a defective cloud machine? To combat this problem the *Guild* introduced an annual MOT test for all machines over three years old. The test would be carried out by Black, Black & Blackemore's in deeper Salford. As with the introduction of licences there was, initially, opposition, but in time it was adopted and the benefits both to safety and insurance cover came to be seen as advantageous.

In the 70s the *Silver Lining Club* was established at Wythenshawe as a place for cloud owners to socialise with colleagues and it proved to be popular with those living in the locality but not so much for those who had to travel long distances. To increase its popularity, a monthly dance was arranged and this had sealed its viability and, to some extent, its notoriety. In the same decade, recognition for outstanding service became the focus for the *Guild,* resulting in a hierarchical system of *commendations, mentions in cloud dispatches* and the *Cloud Defence Medal.* These forms of recognition have become highly regarded in the world of weather and examples were on show in the room.

As many of the original crews got older, the *Guild* started to take a greater interest in their welfare and after protracted negotiations; a rest home was established in Grange-over-Sands called the *Head in the Sky* but its residents affectionately referred to it as the *Halfway House.* The home catered for retired crews who could not face the prospect of retirement alone but owners could also take a break there. It was a most pleasant place and its regular residents enjoyed the frequent visits by current crews who kept them up to date with weather matters.

In the 90s the *Guild's Annual Weather Making Awards* (GAWMAs) were instituted, eight in total and a presentation is held on St.Swithin's Day (July 15th) in the *Silver Lining Club.* These awards have always been regarded with a degree of scepticism but they are, nevertheless, well supported. Most crews accepted that they had a novelty value and the presentation ceremony was always worth attending just for the humour that it inspired. It was not regarded, however, as one of the *Guild's* best ideas.

Coming up to the twenty-first century, the biggest story had been the establishment of the *Weather Making Research Centre* at Llanbedr as part of the *University of Northern England's Department of Weather*. It was early days in terms of advanced research but much was hoped for from this establishment. Seven Faculties had been established each with its own remit. Areas of investigation include *Cloud Making, Cloud Removal, Rain Making, Thunder & Lightning, Snow & Sleet, Wind* and *Special Effects*. The Centre had an ambitious number of weather forms to work on and the world, or at least Wythenshawe Weather Centre, was waiting with interest to see what would emerge from Llanbedr.

The Main Hall

Time was going on and Cirrus, along with his Flight Engineer, was not going to take everything in on this first visit to the museum; there was too much to interest them. They decided to skip the library, cinema and education centre and finish with the main hall but it was doubtful whether they would be able to take in everything there. It was full of all kinds of weather-related memorabilia. Paintings and pictures adorned the walls and models abounded, but the initial focus of the crew of the *Nimbus* would be the examples of cloud machines and mock-ups of the interiors.

The crew of the *Nimbus* headed for the example of one of the first machines used by the RAF Cloud Corps. It had the same bullet-shaped fuselage as the current models but was somewhat smaller. The first obvious difference was the propeller on the front attached to the engine and the rotor blades on top. It also had wings and a fin and looked more like an aeroplane than a cloud machine. Around the fuselage there were several grill-covered holes. These were the holes into which its own cloud would be sucked to go into the onboard condenser. The entry door was on the port side and was padlocked from the outside. The craft sat on its fixed undercarriage which meant that access through the entry door could only be gained via a ladder.

Hanging from the main hall ceiling was another example of an early cloud machine, which enabled Cirrus and Puffy to observe the location of the atomiser and some grill- covered holes out of which the product of the onboard condensers could be dispensed – namely, rain. It was most fascinating for the *Nimbus* crew who had never previously seen an example of the first machines in use.

Attention now turned to the example of a current model for a comparison. Gone were the wings and fin and the rotor blades on top. The fuselage had the same basic shape but was larger. Gone was the propeller and engine in the nose, replaced by four fan duct motors, two on each side and each mounted on a ball joint so that they could be moved up, down, left and right. Saddle tanks to store water were mounted on the curved fuselage sides. A periscope on top of the fuselage had a TV camera mounted inside it and there were many antennae fixed in different places. The undercarriage was now retractable, although no-one ever bothered retracting it in practice. A box- like arrangement on top housed emergency parachutes. Many small holes around the fuselage allowed cloud to be sucked into the condensers as in the early model. The entry door was mounted in the same place as on the early machines but the padlock had been dispensed with. Instead, a side mounted keyboard allowed the crew to gain entry. Pressing the right combination automatically opened the door and an access ladder automatically deployed. The crew of the *Nimbus* was familiar with all this but the comparison was interesting.

A current model hung from the ceiling, enabling the underside to be viewed. The atomiser was still there as were the grill-covered holes through which rain would be dispensed. In addition there were grill-covered loudspeakers from which thunder could pour forth and a sinister looking metal plate to which an onboard electrical generator could apply an electrical charge, so large that a bolt of lightning could be created down to earth.

"That was interesting, Puffy. Perhaps we should now take a look inside a mock-up of each model. Have we got enough time?"

"I think we have, skipper but we better not loiter too much."

With that the two fascinated weather-makers entered the internal mock-up of one of the wartime machines.

On entry into the vintage craft, the first things they noticed was the stowage position for an access ladder and a sliding bolt on the inside of the door to keep it closed, all rather crude and an arrangement which would not comply with modern day health and safety regulations. The inside of the fuselage was just an empty shell apart from the cockpit at the front end. What was striking was that there was no toilet, no washing facilities and no galley. There was a pee tube and it was not screened off in any way.

In the cockpit there was the usual array of flight and engine instruments on the flight deck but the most striking thing was the large compass for navigation. The Flight Engineer's position had a chart table and a radio transmitter/receiver but other than that it was pretty bare. There was a cloud on/off control and a five position selector that enabled the crew to create drizzle, light rain, heavy rain, a short downpour or none of these things, just a cloud.

Cirrus and Puffy decided that they would visit the mock-up interior of a current machine just to remind themselves of how far development had progressed. On stepping into the mock-up, the first thing they were aware of was the panel of buttons which allowed the crew to automatically retract the access ladder and close the machine's door. The fuselage was packed with a variety of equipment running down from the cockpit to the stern of the craft: a toilet, washing facilities, storage refrigerators, a sublimator to convert ice into cloud, a mixer to give clouds colour and a luminance system to make clouds glow. There was also a thunder player which was linked into a Van-de-Graf generator which created lightning. Health and safety was everywhere. Fire extinguishers, smoke detectors, oxygen masks, first aid kits and stowage points for parachutes and life jackets were all clearly on display or marked by signs. It was a massive leap forward from the past.

The cockpit was far more sophisticated than that of the early machines although many of the flight instruments remained the same. What was new was the Identification Beacon, the Plan Position Indicator, the Vertical Separation Indicator, the Global Position System and the early form of navigation aid – the Soakometer. The same level of sophistication applied to the Flight Engineer's station. The same chart table was used but the panel of instruments facing the engineer was an impressive array of dials and controls which allowed weather of all forms to be created. A modern set of communications equipment contrasted with a Morse key, but to signal using a winking cloud demanded it.

Within the cockpit area there was a galley, and a drop down double bunk was fitted into the starboard side of the fuselage. These facilities enabled a crew to conduct weather jobs that lasted several weeks, which made them extremely versatile.

Time was running out and Cirrus, together with his Flight Engineer, just had to leave. There was just too much to see in the museum in one go and a second visit would have to be put into the crew's diary. It would have been most interesting to delve into the library, view some old film in the cinema, not to mention looking in on the education centre, but these would all have to wait. The museum had, however, proved most interesting and informative.

When the crew of the *Nimbus* left the Cloud Museum they were a lot more knowledgeable about the background and history of their field of work. There was a tradition to uphold and from now on they could go anywhere and rain with pride.

A TALE OF TWO CRESS

A ngus McClagg was a proud Scotsman from the Island of Mull. He was a great traditionalist and he exhibited the fact by wearing a kilt at all times and he had a warlike beard of some length. His family's ties with Scotland went back many generations. With other like-minded locals, he took a dram on a Saturday night at the village pub and regaled everyone with some splendid bagpipe playing.

Angus was not a man you would wish to get on the wrong side of; he had a fierce temper, especially on a Saturday night. His vivacious and beautiful daughter, Flora, was the desire of all the young men of Mull but none could contemplate a good relationship with her father and Flora had to fish for a man further afield. In spite of all this, there was no shortage of Mull suitors on a Saturday night after a dram or two, but nothing ever came of it after Angus had put both his bagpipes and his best foot down.

Surprisingly, Angus had a passion for growing watercress and he had a reputation that stretched across Scotland, but not just for growing watercress. He held the Mull record for the number of Police Officers it took to hold him down on a Saturday night.

"Ach man. Yer nae telling mae that Angus grews the watercress. A cannae believe it!"

That was a statement that most local folk tended to make when they got to know about Angus's passion.

The secret of growing the best water cress was a close kept secret but at least two ingredients had leaked out. Angus lived in a village called Salen and close by is Loch Ba which was the source of pure water that he filled his cress tanks with. He added various ingredients but would reveal to no-one what they were, but a certain malt whisky was involved.

The high spot of the year for Angus McClagg was the annual *Oban Fresh Food Gathering* and his famous watercress had won many awards there over the years. His lovely daughter, Flora, had always accompanied him along with her mother until she had passed away. It was at one of the *Gatherings* that Flora had met Seamus. Seamus was Sean O'Leary's son. They came from Bangor in Northern Ireland and Sean had something in common with Flora's father; he had a passion for watercress. It was the passion for watercress that was responsible for the passion Flora felt for Seamus and she was anxious to capitalise on it.

Sean, like Angus, only used a certain source of water for growing his watercress and added some unknown ingredients, but one was an Irish whiskey. For a number of years the top award for watercress at the *Oban Fresh Food Gathering* had gone to either Angus McClagg or Sean O'Leary. Their reputations had gone around the restaurants of Europe and they both made a reasonable living out of their passion.

Flora was especially keen for her father to win this year's top award for she thought it would give her some kudos that may be useful in terms of cementing a relationship with Seamus. She had secretly been writing to him for some time and looked forward to her next visit to Oban with great anticipation. The feeling was mutual. Ever since Seamus had met Flora he was smitten with her and she always looked special when she appeared at the *Gathering* in her Scottish attire. She stood out in any gathering; Oban was no exception.

The date of the *Gathering* was getting closer and Angus was especially keen to win the top award as a result of a bad bout of vanity and the constant mithering by his daughter, and he was spending all the time he could gloating and nurturing the watercress in his special tanks.

"Angus, yae dunna think that the cress isnae as good as last year do yer?" asked one of his drinking pals who had called in to see him.

Angus made a close inspection of his crop and most frustratingly he had to agree.

"What do yer put it doon too Angus?"

That was a difficult question to answer but an answer had to be found. Drawing on his extensive water cress experience, Angus remembered that in previous years, if he used the water from Loch Ba when it had fallen below a certain level he would not get the best results. This year had been one of the driest for a long time. Maybe he ought to go and take a look at the Loch's level.

An inspection of Loch Ba confirmed what Angus had suspected. The Loch level was lower than usual; it needed topping up. But how?

Over a dram in the pub Angus got to discussing the level of Loch Ba and how it was creating a bit of a problem for him.

"Angus do yer remember the time when the big croose liner sailed frae Oban to St.Kilda?" remarked the pub landlord.

"Aye, ah do that but what has that tae doo with Loch Ba?"

"Well they took a lassie wee em that had crashed on St.Kilda in a clood machine."

"Och aye. I remember that noo."

"Well can yae nae get in touch with the clood machine people an see what they can doo fer yae?"

With that seed planted in the mind of Angus he went away home and asked Flora to work her miracles with the internet and find out what he wanted to know. Within an hour she had not only found the details of Wythenshawe Weather Centre but she had also been in contact and got a quote to get a supply of suitable water delivered to top up the Loch.

"Och Flora, what would ah do withooot yer?" said Angus, embracing his daughter at the same time.

In Bangor a certain Sean O'Leary was having exactly the same problem. His watercress was distinctly lacklustre and he had to do something about it. A conversation with a friend brought about the notion that he had been here before and like Angus he went off to inspect his water source.

Lough Mourne, just north of Carrickfergus, was the secret water source of Northern Ireland's premier watercress grower, Sean O'Leary, and as with Loch Ba it was much lower than usual. The long dry summer was being experienced by the whole of Great Britain and Sean needed to find a solution. He talked to his son Seamus and immediately Seamus reminded his father of Aurora Cloudealis.

"Now what in heavens name has Aurora got to do with it and who is she anyway?"

"Aurora Cloudealis is not a girl, father, it was a special display that was put on at Portrush by a team of cloud machines."

"Well why are you telling me this, Seamus?"

"I was thinking that you might try contacting the cloud machines and seeing if they can't bring some rain over."

"Well that may not be such a bad idea but how can I get in touch with a cloud?"

At this juncture an exasperated Seamus went away to find out what he could on the internet before contacting Wythenshawe Weather Centre to make enquiries.

"Here you are father; I have a quote telling you how much it would cost to rain on Lough Mourne."

Sean couldn't believe what his son had done but he was most pleased and placed an arm around his shoulder to thank him before saying – *"but it's still your round next."*

At Home in Slaidburn

The kitchen window of the Cumulus home in Slaidburn was wide open, letting in on a sunny day the sounds of the countryside. Birds sang and the leaves on the trees rustled in harmony whilst the warm breeze provided a chorus. The odd butterfly took a peek inside along with one or two bees, but they got a less welcome reception as Puffy wafted them out with the aid of a tea towel. It was one of those days that made Puffy feel at peace with the world and he continued enjoying the feeling until the postman and the newspaper boy entered the drive.

Having collected the post and the Daily Gloom at the front door, Puffy delivered them, along with a tray of coffee and a bacon butty, to the lounge where his skipper, Cirrus Cumulus, or to give him the title he preferred, Captain Cumulus, sat daydreaming.

"Morning, skipper," began Puffy. *"Here's your morning coffee and the post."*

"No paper then this morning, Puffy?"

"So there is, skipper, that as well."

With that, Puffy made a discreet tactical withdrawal.

It was not long before Cirrus could be heard shouting to himself.

"Whose side are these judges on I want to know? Its damned madness, that's what it is!"

For once, Puffy couldn't contain himself. He had to find out what his skipper thought was so crazy and he popped into the lounge to join him.

With an audience, even if it was only of one, it was enough to trigger a further outburst.

"You know I really don't get it. I read time and again how innocent people get burgled and when they attempt to defend themselves or prevent the burglar from getting away or stealing something, they get prosecuted for doing it. That can't be right. What do these judges think they are doing?"

"They say they are upholding the law, skipper," replied Puffy.

"Well if that's the case, the law is not working in our interest and it needs changing or it needs some common sense using when it is being interpreted."

Puffy felt confident that he could contribute to this discussion and for once he felt he wanted to.

"They can't change the law without the agreement of the EU these days."

That was a sore point with his skipper whose blood pressure started to rise.

"Damned European Union! Membership of that money-sucking organisation will be the downfall of our independence. The sooner we get out the sooner we can govern ourselves properly again."

"Phew skipper! You really do have strong feelings about the EU."

"You mark my words, Puffy, if the EU gets its way it will see the weather-making business go the same way as our fishing industry."

That clearly meant down the pan!

Cirrus, now in full flow, turned his venom on the law profession.

"In my father's day, the law profession was held in high esteem but no longer is that the case. All these firms encouraging claims for this, that and the other are changing all that and they are making a fortune out of crime with what they charge in fees. Just look at what they have been paid for free legal aid by the Government. The legal profession is probably the only profession that has a vested interest in crime continuing. It's big business for them."

Puffy could see that his skipper was well and truly into one of his more reflective moods and mischievously threw in a little bait.

"I agree, skipper, and when someone is convicted of a crime it costs a fortune to keep them in prison."

"Now that's another thing, Puffy. Look at all these murderers that we are paying to keep. In times of austerity like now, we can't afford the luxury of providing for these evil villains. What really makes my blood boil is that the

Government can justify spending huge sums of money each year to look after someone in prison but can't afford to invest in paying the fees for a young person to be educated in a university. One's an investment and the other is a liability. I really am beginning to despair about our politicians."

Cirrus sat back in his favourite chair and took a breather from the problems of his beloved country, and a momentary lapse from thinking and talking allowed him to enjoy the ray of sunshine that had exercised its right to light up a portion of his lounge. In the process of doing this, the sun had illuminated a picture of the machine that Cirrus and his faithful engineer had had many weather adventures aboard – the *Nimbus*. Puffy followed his skipper's eyes and could tell from the smile on his face that he was enjoying what he saw.

"I think we should take another job on, Puffy. Don't you agree?"

"Aye, aye skipper, I do."

"Let me have the post will you. There maybe something interesting in it."

Puffy had already brought the post in but duly picked it up again and gave it to his Captain. Cirrus quickly opened one or two letters and just as quickly confined them to the rubbish basket as was quite common nowadays. One item he did not dispose of in this manner was the latest copy of the *Monthly Downpour*, the journal that kept all members of '*The Guild of Cloud Owners*' up to date with what was happening in the cloud world. It took some time to wade through all the information but he was drawn to a notice that informed members that a fair amount of work was currently available and members should either visit Wythenshawe Weather Centre or call the Superintendent's Secretary, Miss Joanne Black.

"Puffy, get Goldilocks on the phone will you. There's some work available."

Talking About Work

When Cirrus Cumulus was busy making enquiries about new work that had come in to Wythenshawe Weather Centre, he was not the only one.

Wally Lenticular and his Flight Engineer, Bert Drummond, crew of the *Discovery*, had also been browsing through the latest edition of *The Monthly Downpour* in Wally's palatial Lakeland home. The two of them were busy discussing whether to take on some new work but kept getting distracted by the comings and goings of Wally's dinky young housemaid, Felicity, who they found wonderfully enticing. It was the third trip Felicity had made at the joint request of Wally and Bert and she started to get suspicious although she had to confess to herself that she didn't really mind all the attention. Nevertheless, the crew of the *Discovery* could not justify asking Felicity to perform another unnecessary errand in order that they could cast their eyes on her feline shape again. They did not want to make their interest too obvious.

"Boss, I think we need to get back aboard the Discovery again and do some work. It's nice to take a break but there's nothing to compare with a mobile office in the sky. This place of yours is lovely and posh, Wally, but it can't beat the ever changing scene that we view when we are delivering weather."

Wally looked at Bert and just smiled in agreement. It was settled and Wally rang Goldilocks.

"Miss Black speaking! How can I help you?"

"Hello, Goldilocks. It's Wally Lenticular here."

It was a little time before Miss Black stopped chuckling to herself and got down to business. The work involved taking water of a particular quality to Northern Ireland to top up a small Lough just north of Carrickfergus. The job was not big or special but there was an emphasis on the water quality and she suggested that Wally should consult his *Compendium of Water Sources* to locate a suitable supply.

A short discussion between the crew of the *Discovery* resulted in Felicity being asked to bring the *Compendium* and she left to find it whilst being tracked by two pairs of male eyeballs. It was too good to be resisted. The same two sets of eyeballs tracked her return but attention eventually turned to the *Compendium* in search of a source of water that would match that contained in Lough Mourne. Page after page was scoured in an attempt to find a source and especially one reasonably close by. Eventually, it was decided that Anglezarke reservoir, north-west of Bolton in Lancashire would be ideal. In spite of the long summer it was still full and it had a sufficient supply to act as a top-up source and its contents were as near a match as was possible to get. With the research done, Wally contacted Miss Black to tell her that he would take the job on for Sean O'Leary and the deal was sealed. Felicity returned to collect the *Compendium* and both Bert and his skipper returned to admiring her presence and much regretted her departure.

"Do you think we should ask for a coffee, skipper?"

Cirrus and Puffy arrived at Wythenshawe Weather Centre to check the *Nimbus* over and ensure that they had adequate supplies on board for the job they had just taken on. It was something of a surprise, but a pleasant one, to find Wally and his Flight Engineer, Bert Drummond, doing the same thing.

"What have you got on, Wally?" asked Cirrus.

"I'm off to Northern Ireland doing a top-up. What about you, Cirrus?"

"Same, but I'm off to Scotland."

Whilst the two skippers talked about work, the two flight engineers conversed about more personal matters.

"How are you getting on with Goldilocks?" enquired Bert.

"To tell you the truth, Bert, I hardly get the chance to get my arm around her what with work and things, but I am going to invite her to Slaidburn as soon as I can."

"Has your divorce come through yet, Puffy?"

That brought the conversation to an abrupt end which was rather like Puffy's marriage. The two flight engineers decided it would be for the best if they just went about their business and this they did.

By the time it was dark both the *Nimbus* and the *Discovery* had been fully checked over and provisioned. They both started up their fan duct motors together and moved out of their allotted parking spots in the huge Wythenshawe hangar before turning to face the closed doors. At this point, with the *Nimbus* leading, the large doors started to open and the lights started to dim. The two machines lined up side by side outside the doors. It was a very dark night due to the overcast sky and both skippers waited for clearance to take off. An agreement had been reached that the *Nimbus* should be first to ascend and, when clearance was given by Wythenshawe control, it ascended into the darkness rapidly to clear the flight path into Manchester Airport which passed directly overhead of the Weather Centre. The *Nimbus* didn't stop ascending until it reached 5,000 feet at which height it hovered momentarily whilst Cirrus switched on the ID beacon and entered the latitude and longitude of his destination into his Soakometer/navaid.

It was a murky night to be making a flight. The cloud base was at 2,000 feet and it extended all the way up to 10,000 feet. The only view of the ground that the crew of the *Nimbus* would get tonight would be on the flight deck pop-up TV screen aided by the image on the Plan Position Indicator. Cirrus checked his watch and then opened the throttles to begin the short flight to the water source that would be atomised and taken in cloud form to the Island of Mull.

An hour later, the *Nimbus* arrived over Anglezarke reservoir and Cirrus brought his cloud machine to a hover before descending in the overcast. At 2,000 feet the *Nimbus* emerged from the night cloud and the reservoir came in to view. A break in the cloud to the west allowed the light reflected off the moon to illuminate the surface of the water which threw into stark relief the shore line that gave the reservoir its distinctive shape. The *Nimbus* ceased descending at 1,500 feet and Cirrus suggested to Puffy that they have a cup of tea and enjoy the vista for ten minutes before proceeding to steal the contents of the beauty that lay below them. Puffy heartily agreed and put the kettle on in the galley.

Cirrus had noticed on his flight to Anglezarke that there was a blip on his PPI that had been following the *Nimbus*. He didn't think it was of much significance until it practically overlapped his own blip in the centre of the PPI screen. Cirrus peered out of the cockpit window into the darkness to see what it could be. It was difficult to see anything but as the gap in the cloud widened in the west to let more moonlight in he suddenly picked the object out.

"Well I'll be blowed! It looks like Wally has followed us here."

Puffy came forward from the galley to take a look at what all the excitement was about.

"What's he doing here?" asked Puffy.

"I don't know but get him on the radio; I'm going to speak to him."

"What the devil are you doing here, Wally?"

"I could just as well ask you the same thing, Cirrus."

"I was here first, Wally, so don't beat about the bush."

Wally went on to explain that he was here to atomise the water in the reservoir and take it in cloud form to Northern Ireland.

"You can't do that. I'm here to do the same thing. If we both steal the reservoir it'll be empty and that will lead to an uproar."

Wally paused and thought for a moment or two before replying.

"Suppose we both take half of what we want from Anglezarke and then slide across to Yarrow and take the other half from there."

Yarrow reservoir was adjacent to Anglezarke and although smaller in surface area, it is significantly deeper.

Cirrus mused over this suggestion and looked at Puffy who gave a nod of agreement. There was a question of water quality but considering that the contents of Yarrow overflow into Anglezarke it shouldn't be a problem.

"Ok, Wally. Let's do that. You fill up from Yarrow first whilst I take Anglezarke and then we can swop over."

"Okey dokey, Cirrus."

The two cloud machines spent the next thirty minutes atomising water and creating clouds around themselves. Two Cumberland Greys steadily formed over the top of two Lancashire reservoirs and each fell in level at the same time, but no-one in the night was aware of it. The *Nimbus* and *Discovery* swopped reservoirs and continued atomising but this time the stolen reservoir was either stored in the machines' saddle tanks or frozen before being stored in their numerous refrigerators. At the end of all this the *Nimbus* headed north to Scotland whilst the *Discovery* headed north-west to Northern Ireland. If the two skippers had taken the trouble to consult their *Compendium of Water Sources* they would know that Yarrow reservoir was filled with water of a much inferior quality to that of Anglezarke but it was too late for that now.

Back at 5,000 feet each machine made its journey through nature's clag. Around midday the Cumberland Greys broke free from the stratus that had been hanging over the country for sometime but the journey was slow and laborious against the prevailing wind. The *Nimbus* arrived over Mull early the following evening and Cirrus decided they would have a meal before raining on Loch Ba. Angus McClagg had no idea that the cloud above was to be his water cress salvation but had a feeling that since it was going nowhere it might be what he had paid for. Anyway, if he was going to win anything at Oban it better get on with the job and fast.

There was no rushing Cirrus when he could smell the meal Puffy was cooking in the galley. There was a time and place for everything and right now it was time to eat over Loch Ba. With the meal over, the crew of the *Nimbus* set about raining on the Loch and they did it in style with a downpour. Within an hour of the end of the downpour, Angus was filling up the tank behind his tractor to take back to his water- cress farm and top up his cress filled tanks.

Now that should be a winning liquid, thought Angus, before adding a bottle of malt whisky to each tank.

The *Nimbus* could now start the journey back down the west coast as a somewhat depleted Cumberland Grey made up of a blend of two different reservoirs. Another twenty-four hours and the crew would be back at home in Slaidburn.

Wally and Bert had a similar experience on board the *Discovery* with the exception that Sean was not present to witness their downpour on Lough Mourne. Bert had to contact Wythenshawe to get them to let Sean know that his water source had been replenished. When Sean received the information he set out with his tanker to bring some of his supply to Bangor and then topped his cress tanks up before adding to each a bottle of Irish whiskey.

Serious Competition at Oban

Oban Fresh Food Gathering in 2013 was extremely well supported. Folk had flocked here from the Western Isles bringing with them the best they had grown with great care. Stall after stall exhibited a variety of home-grown produce that created an enticing smell that gave character to the *Gathering*. Old friendships were rekindled and a spirit of good humour permeated the scene.

"Hello, Angus. How are you? asked Sean.

"Ach, I'm fine, Sean, and how are you?"

Pleasantries exchanged, the two passionate watercress growers got to talking about their current crops and the difficulties the year had brought whilst casting an eye at the same time on each other's display. Both had brought water-cress that looked exceedingly healthy and each had a distinct aroma. Indeed the aroma was slightly intoxicating and each of their stands witnessed the gathering of a number of visitors who loitered just to experience it.

Whilst Angus and Sean admired each others work, their offspring admired each other. Flora looked exquisite in her Scottish attire whilst Seamus was slightly scruffy, but they looked at each other in the most desiring of ways. Seamus knew, however, that Flora's father was a man of no mean disposition and the whole of his Irish charm would be required if he was to steal his daughter away for a time.

The number of inquisitive folk gathered around the stalls of the two watercress growers was beginning to get embarrassing, especially as they all seemed to be getting a little inebriated. It was to be hoped that the judges would not be under any undue influence.

As the time for the judging got nearer, Seamus saw an opportunity to grab a few moments with Flora and the pair of them sneaked off to a more private corner of the location that housed the *Gathering*.

"It's lovely to see you again, Flora."

"Aye an it's lovely to see you, Seamus too."

The small talk continued until Seamus's Irish instinct told him it was time to embrace her, which he did. Flora had no intentions of being outdone by an Irish embrace and added to it with Scottish passion that took the wind out of Seamus, but it didn't impact on the Irish arm around her slender waist. Stage two in the process is traditionally a kiss and, being traditionalists, they duly complied. They then moved on to stage three but that's too private to comment on, although there were one or two casual observers who went on to take notes.

The judges visited the watercress grown by Angus first, but they were having difficulty getting through the throng of inebriated bystanders not all of whom were standing by this stage in the proceedings. Several burly security guards had to be called for to carve a way through and, being of an athletic nature, the kilt-wearing guards removed a number of bodies with vigour until the judges finally got access to the watercress that was creating all the fuss. Angus stood proudly at the side of his watercress bearing stall and looked most impressive. His *Tam o' shanter* went well with his long but neatly trimmed beard and, with his shoulders back, he had the bearing of a true champion.

The judges looked at the watercress grown by Angus from all angles before handling it. Throughout the judging the aroma given off by the cress was proving to be most enjoyable and the judges judged for an exceptionally long period, much to the pleasure of Angus and the displeasure of Sean, who was following the scene with some consternation. Eventually, after a little swaying, the judges stood up straight and looked on in horror as the water cress started to wilt. They tried a sample of it before it wilted too much and were horrified by its obnoxious taste. Angus watched all that was happening in total disbelief and started to speculate on who could have sabotaged his award-winning cress.

"Ach aye, al swear this is tha best yar faer watter cress smelling," remarked one judge.

"Noo doot aboot it but its nae good faer eatin," was the reply by another but the third judge could only reply with a loud belch.

Looking at watercress and then feeling it under the eyes of its grower, Sean O'Leary, the three judges, taking in ever increasing amounts of the intoxicating aroma, began to wilt and then Sean's cress did the same thing. Looking on in amazement, the judges tried a quick sample and found it just as obnoxious as the last. The intoxicating aroma took its toll and when it came time to leave, the judges only managed it with the aid of the guards and some wheelchairs.

"Ach I have never seen judges like it afore," remarked Angus to his fellow contestant, Sean, who had to agree with him and added, *"But what happened to our water cress?"*

"Ach man! We are truly cressfallen without doot," replied Angus who went on,

"Ah didna do anything different this year, not at all."

"Neither did I," replied Sean.

The judges retired to consider their verdict but there was sleep to be had first after such an intoxicating experience and the delay in announcing the results of their deliberations was not well received.

Angus and Sean stood and glared at their wilting watercress but the cress did not respond, it just carried on wilting and, as it did so, the intoxicating aroma was replaced by one of rotting vegetation. Bystanders gathered to point and jeer and sniff the new unpleasant smell before making a hasty departure.

No man would have any desire to showcase rotting watercress at the *Oban Fresh Food Gathering* but that's what Angus and Sean had to do until the judges reappeared, and it was not pleasant. Being surrounded by a distinct stink was beginning to wilt the two watercress growers and they were only saved by the return of the three judges. Looking as if they were suffering from a hangover, they quickly delivered their unanimous verdict – the contest for the best watercress was to go to Rab Dundonald from Lochinvar. Angus and Sean came nowhere for the first time in over ten years and they did not enjoy defeat.

The only saving grace for the McClagg and O'Leary families this year was the cementing of Scottish – Irish relations. Flora and Seamus had progressed to stage five in the lover's manual and a new addition to the family would be on the scene in due course.

"Seamus, yae shood of stuck with the cress," remarked Angus, but it would be handy to have someone extra to help with the growing next year, he thought.

A few days later when Cirrus was getting back into his usual horizontal position on the settee in his Slaidburn lounge, Puffy came in to tell him that Mr Spite was on the phone.

"Hello, Mr Spite, its Captain Cumulus here."

"Cirrus, can you tell me where you got the water from that you took to Mull?"

A question put like that was ominous, thought Cirrus. Maybe it would be best, perhaps, to stick with the one source, Anglezarke reservoir, and that's the answer he gave.

"Well in that case, Cirrus, did you consult The Compendium of Water Sources *to check that it was a match for Loch Ba?"*

"Yes I did," replied Cirrus who went on, *"Is there a problem?"*

"It appears to be a bad case of wilted cress and Angus is trying to get to the bottom of it. Thanks anyway. Cheerio."

It might not have been such a good idea after all blending water from two different sources, thought Cirrus, but he also thought it best to keep quiet about it.

Skipper, there's another phone call for you."

"Who is it this time?"

"It's Wally Lenticular."

"Put him on."

"Cirrus, I have just had the strangest call from Mr Spite!"

CLOUDTANIC

E ddie Stormbart was a shrewd businessman with friends in high places. He had long been connected with the world of weather-making, and his cloud convoys, ploughing along the roads in the sky to far flung places, on Government work, were known around the world.

It was during a night out in his local pub that Eddie had first thought about the melting pole caps and the rising sea levels. He had thought how absurd that was when many countries faced the impossible challenge of growing crops due to long droughts. One part of the world had too much and another part too little.

Some of Eddie's acquaintances lived a life of politics and some were feeling the wrath of their constituents when it came to doling out foreign aid. This was the subject that finally crystallised Eddie's dream. Thinking out loud, Eddie posed the idea of taking the world's excess water to drought-ridden places using cloud machines, and his audience stopped drinking to drink in the words they had just heard. Being politicians, their first thought was money. If Eddie's idea had any merit then it could solve two problems in one go, and instead of giving aid in the form of money, they could do it with rain. Not only that, the funds could be diverted to paying the cloud machines, which would keep the money in the UK economy and that should take away a lot of the pressure the economy was currently experiencing. A further bonus was that they could probably get away with paying out less.

Eddie found himself being bombarded with questions about the feasibility of his idea but he could only suggest, at this moment in time, that he needed to put more work into it.

"Jolly good idea that man Stormbart came up with," said the prime minister over tea at number ten.

"I'm glad you think so PM," replied the foreign affairs minister.

"You know, it would be helpful to provide rain aid rather than pay aid. It would be one way of ensuring that money doesn't fall into the wrong hands."

"I agree entirely, PM."

"If we got this idea in our next manifesto, it would do the party a lot of good in the next general election, don't you think?"

"Absolutely, PM. A wizard idea!"

"Perhaps we could get this chap Stormbart to accept a quarter of what we have been paying out and that would go down well with the electorate as well."

The foreign affairs minister felt somewhat uncomfortable with the suggestion of offering such a small proportion of the government's potential savings to an idea that had so much going for it politically, and the PM picked up on it.

"Look, if this chap Stormbart has any misgivings about helping us with this, just dangle the prospect of a knighthood in front of him. That should do the trick."

For several weeks after this discussion, the PM had extolled the virtues of the wisdom of his government to any section of the media that cared to listen and any idea of keeping any plan secret until it had been proved workable was cast aside. This had been how Eddie, at some time in the past, had come to be involved in foreign aid. For the sake of his own credibility he felt obliged to come up with something that was workable.

The mechanics involved in taking water from a place in which there was an excess to a place in which there was a dire shortage took a considerable time to deal with. Eddie worked out that approximately twenty-five fully loaded cloud machines could provide a useful monsoon to an arable area the size of a town like Bolton. The real problem was that the fuel required by the fan duct motors on each machine to fly the distances involved, only allowed the cloud machines to carry half their rain-making capacity. Even with half a load, those involved would have to stop half way to refuel and that's how Gibraltar came into the equation.

No matter how Eddie had looked at the problem he could not get away from the fact that he would have to double the number of cloud machines required and, apart from the difficulty of getting fifty machines to work for him, there was the question of cost.

On this latter point he had no need to be concerned. The government had by now committed itself to a policy of non-proliferation of sea water, due to melting polar caps, and to providing a rich source of crop growing fluid for drought-ridden countries. Whilst this was a tall order, it placed the UK on the world stage of influence for which there was unlimited funding.

Government money flowed into the bank account of Eddie Stormbart who proceeded with a huge recruitment drive to acquire the services of fifty or so cloud machine operators, and an advertisement appeared in the Monthly Downpour for a whole year. Each accepted candidate signed a contract to work for '**Stormbart's Weather Solutions**' which, unlike their current arrangements, guaranteed a regular income. That was a particularly attractive proposition for some of the cloud machine owners and initially they accepted the routine involved with working for Eddie.

Taking water from places where there was an excess to places where there was a shortage was not such an exciting thing to do. A typical job would involve fifty machines, or more, heading out to a rendezvous with Eddie in the polar region to atomise water and then convey it in convoy to some place and rain, not forgetting a short refuelling stop in Gibraltar. Then it was back home for a few days before starting again, and each of these jobs usually lasted between four and six weeks at a time.

After a while, the routine of foreign aid got quite boring. Living in the confined space of a cloud machine for up to six weeks and with little variety on the cooking front was enough to drive crews insane, but the income made it palatable.

The time had come, however, when it was becoming exceedingly frustrating for Eddie to round up the fifty or so machines that he needed for a specific job. There were always the few machines that had maintenance work being done on them or that were undergoing an MOT test. Occasionally, a crew would back out due to sickness; all this was usual and to be expected. The problem was getting worse, however, and it was getting more difficult to round up the required numbers, and the problem was exacerbated by an increasing number of machines dropping out of a convoy after a few days with either a technical problem or some form of sickness. Things simply couldn't carry on like this for much longer. The strain on Eddie was beginning to tell.

Time for a Rethink

Making a rare visit to Wythenshawe Weather Centre, Eddie took the opportunity of discussing his current worries with his long time friend Ivor Spite, the Superintendent in charge. Eddie was privileged to use the Superintendent's first name. To everyone else, he was Mr I.N.Spite CDM.

"You need a new kind of cloud machine, a much bigger one and there is only one place to go to get that!"

Eddie knew what was coming next.

"Black, Black & Blackemore's have an excellent design team. They could manufacture the machine you are looking for and that would help to solve your current problem."

That was the solution that Eddie had already reached but it made him feel better that someone else had reached the same conclusion as well.

Thanking Ivor for his time, Eddie departed, but not before taking a good look at Goldilocks as he left. *What a stunner for a secretary,* he thought but he was more motivated by his current problem and departed quickly.

The design team at Black, Black & Blackemore's sat around the big table in the company boardroom to thrash out with Eddie his requirements for a new machine.

"Mr Stormbart," began John Chadwick, the company's head of design. *"As I understand it, you wish to convey your current amount of water overseas using half the machines that you currently use. Am I correct in assuming that?"*

"Yes, that's correct, Mr Chadwick."

The head of design went on, *"The machines currently subcontracted to you can only carry half of their potential load due to the extra fuel required to power their engines.*

If we could fit new, more powerful, and fuel efficient engines, like the ones we fitted on the Nimbus II, all these machines could then double their carrying potential."

At this point several of the gathered design team began to make calculations on their computers and, after quite some time, they unanimously agreed that even with the new engines, a fuel stopover at Gibraltar would still be required.

The design team was already toying with the idea of designing a bigger machine that could carry enough fuel to eliminate the need for any refuelling stop and Eddie jumped in at this juncture in the proceedings.

"If a bigger machine was built to accommodate more fuel, would it not be possible to include more water storage tanks and refrigerators?"

The discussion then turned to the notion of using bigger clouds instead of carrying more water and ice to top the cloud up as it rained off on mother earth. After a somewhat heated debate, it was agreed that juggerclouds would not generally be accepted and the idea of using normal sized clouds, topped up with onboard supplies when it was making rain, would be a far more acceptable solution.

The head of design, acting as chairman, then brought matters to an end.

"Gentlemen, I think we need to conclude things at this point. What we need to do is to come up with a design that meets Mr Stormbart's requirements. We also need to carefully look at the new fan duct motors under design to see if our power requirements can be met."

There was general agreement with Mr Chadwick and, once a date had been agreed to reconvene, everyone got up to leave.

Several days after the meeting, Eddie bumped into Cirrus Cumulus in Wythenshawe's cavernous hangar and a conversation struck up regarding Eddie's requirement for a new machine. It was the talking point of the centre. Nothing could be kept secret here for long.

"It all boils down to the right motors being available," commented Eddie who went on, *"If they are, then a much bigger machine could be made that can carry more much further."*

Cirrrus pondered for a moment and then remarked, *"But what about the crew? They could be on a job for weeks. They would need more facilities."*

"We haven't got round to that yet, Cirrus."

"You would only need half the machines you currently use," commented Cirrus.

"Well that's the object. I'm having a huge problem getting the numbers together at present and it's doing my head in!"

The design team at Black, Black & Blackemore's in deeper Salford used all their design skills to come up with something that met all of the requirements laid down at the first meeting. Using CAD (Computer Aided Design) techniques, they had worked furiously to arrive at a suitable design but they had been greatly helped by the very latest fan duct motors that more than met their needs. The results of all this work would be put to Mr Stormbart at the next meeting.

The model in the middle of the boardroom table quite took away Eddie's breath. It was the same length and shape as the cloud machines in current use but the fuselage was clearly that of a double-deck version. Other than that, it was outwardly similar.

John Chadwick began proceedings by describing what the Salford based team had done.

"The key to our design has been provided by these brand new fan duct motors. They may look the same as those on your current machines but, believe me, these are far superior. They produce a far greater power output and are remarkably fuel efficient as well as being silent running."

Mr Chadwick paused at this point to lift the top off the model to reveal the top deck internal details before continuing.

"By providing this upper floor in the machine, it has been possible to increase the number of water storage tanks and the increased size of the fuselage means that the number of saddle tanks on the outside has been increased as well. We have included some refrigerators so that some of the water can be stored as ice. If you look carefully, you can see that extra evaporators have been fitted to convert the water to vapour, or cloud, as you would call it, and also sublimators to convert the stored ice into cloud."

"How much more can be stored?" enquired Eddie.

"This machine can carry four times as much as the present models, that is to say, 16,000,000 gallons."

That figure staggered Eddie who quickly realised that one of these machines could do the work of four of the ones he had subcontracted to him.

Thoughts now turned to crewing one of these mammoth rain-makers.

"There is enough fuel on one of these new models to allow you to fly, fully loaded, around the world without stopping," remarked one of Mr Chadwick's colleagues.

"But I couldn't do that with a crew of two," remarked Eddie.

"That's one of the things we wanted to talk to you about, Mr Stormbart, before we proceed to the next stage of design."

After some discussion it was agreed that the new machine needed to accommodate two crews, making four persons in total. When one crew was working, the other could rest. Clearly, there was some additional design work needed to accommodate them all.

Eddie left the factory in deeper Salford feeling confident that he was getting closer to solving his diminishing cloud machine support that was so essential to meet the government's foreign aid aspirations.

The next visit to Black, Black & Blackemore's factory revealed the final results of the design team's efforts. The model in the middle of the boardroom table looked no different than before but when the top was removed to show the internal fit, it was a different story.

"As you may observe, Mr Stormbart, we have included on this upper deck a sleeping area for four persons in two double bunks and a wash area which includes a shower and toilet. If you look here, you can see a decently equipped galley which will allow the crew members to cook a good meal."

It was interesting to note that a DVD player had also been installed and that would certainly help any crew to pass away some time when not down on the flight deck. Access to the crew section of the upper deck which was situated up forard was by a staircase but it was hard to see properly until the upper deck of the model was removed to reveal the lower deck.

Gone was the double-bunk that was normally stowed in the starboard side of the fuselage. In its place was a staircase to the upper deck. The flight-deck galley had been retained so that a duty crew could make themselves a hot drink and bacon butty or even a pre-prepared meal. It all looked rather splendid and Eddie congratulated the design team on a job well done.

"Well, Mr Stormbart, I can see that you like the results of our work," said Mr Chadwick.

"I do indeed, Mr Chadwick. When can I have one?"

Implications

It was time for Eddie Stormbart to sit down and think about how in the future he would deliver rain on behalf of the government. The new cloud machine on the drawing board at Black, Black & Blackemore's was about to change everything.

Once a good many calculations had been completed, Eddie concluded that future convoys need only consist of thirteen of the new cloud machines, although it would be prudent to have a further two as back-up. There was always going to be a need for maintenance, not to mention the fixing of any malfunctions and, in the future, each machine would require an MOT test in order to ensure that they were up to the standards required to keep their certificate of airworthiness.

Smaller convoys offered a number of advantages, especially in terms of navigation. It had always been a policy of Eddie's to lead each convoy himself. He considered himself to be a master navigator, which was more than can be said of a number of those subcontracted to work for him. Leading a convoy had been one way of ensuring that he minimised the number of cloud machines that he lost en-route to some place. It didn't, however, prevent machines going astray in the dark or when flying through nature's clouds. With the new machines, he could choose to offer work to the best crews that he knew and that would help considerably.

It had also been a policy of Eddie's to keep his crews on their toes during a long journey by getting them to perform CPT (Cloud Physical Training) but he might have to review that. The new machines were a lot larger than the current models and may not lend themselves to it. This was something that would have to be investigated when the first new machine came on line. On the other hand, CPT may not be needed. The crew had a large galley and relaxation area and a DVD player.

It occurred to Eddie at this point that maybe a TV set could be installed and, perhaps, some exercise equipment. The more he thought about this, the more he liked the ideas and he made a note to ring the design team and see if they could be incorporated into the new model.

A few days later, chewing things over with the Superintendent at Wythenshawe, Mr Spite raised a poignant issue that had escaped Eddie.

"You do realise, Eddie, that you won't get fifteen new machines all at one go. It takes time to manufacture these things. More than likely you will get one every three months or so."

Eddie was taken aback by this comment. He had not made any allowance for this. Perhaps he ought to ask Black, Black & Blackemore's to give him some delivery dates. That way he could devise a plan.

The Superintendent continued, *"As I see it, you could either phase these new machines in gradually, or wait until they were all ready for use."*

"I think, on balance, it would be better to integrate them into my convoys as they become available.

"But your convoys will be made up of a combination of machines. Will that not be a problem?"

Eddie thought for a moment and then replied,

"I suppose that the drawback will be that I would still need a refuelling stop and I will still be limited as to how far I can travel at one go but, on the other hand, if there are any problems to iron out with the new machines, this would be the best time to do it. The other thing is that the government is anxious to crack on with this as soon as possible."

Mr Spite had certainly given Eddie something to think about but he couldn't plan anything until he got some concrete, or perhaps that should be cloud, information from the manufacturer. When he did, it confirmed what Mr Spite had suggested. The new machines would be delivered on a three monthly basis. That meant that it would take three years and nine months to replace the existing convoy system with a new one made up of new machines. The question now was how the government would react to that.

A Meeting with Ministers

That's a bit of a blow to our plans, Stormbart," said the PM, heading the ministerial meeting about foreign aid.

"We are already committed to switching from money to rain, and reducing the cost."

Clearly the PM was not impressed and Eddie Stormbart was left feeling distinctly uncomfortable.

The foreign minister felt that he ought to interject to diffuse the PM's displeasure.

"I feel sure, Prime Minister, that the situation can be handled to our advantage. Whilst we may have to introduce our new plans gradually, that need only apply to the delivery of rain. There is nothing to stop the government from ending foreign aid money payments immediately. We can legitimately claim that we are investing the aid in more efficient ways of delivering help of a more practical nature in the future."

That was fine but it didn't get round the fact that some countries that government rain could not reach at present would lose all of their aid. A heated argument then followed between ministers.

"We have an obligation to help nations poorer than ourselves," argued one.

"That may be so, but we can't keep giving money we don't have. The interest we are paying to get the money we give away is astronomical. We can't keep doing it," replied another.

"Prime Minister, we mustn't lose sight of the fact that an enormous amount of the aid funds we provide are being siphoned off for all kinds of illegitimate purposes, including terrorism, and we must put a stop to that."

There was general agreement to this.

Eddie had been silent throughout the ministerial discussion but felt that he could make a constructive contribution. He raised his hand and the chairman of the meeting took note.

"You wish to speak, Mr Stormbart?"

Nervously, Eddie rose to his feet to face the ministers. These were pretty ruthless individuals and he knew he would have to be careful how he phrased things.

"Prime Minister, I know you are concerned about the places your rain cannot reach. When I get my second new machine it would be possible for it to leave the main weather convoy after its initial rain target and carry on to rain wherever you deem appropriate and it would be possible to expand on this as each additional new machine came on line."

Silence fell on the ministers as they drank in this suggestion and the silence was significant, for politicians are not known for being silent. Eventually, the silence was broken when one of them characteristically boomed out, *"Splendid idea, Stormbart! I can just see the face now of one of those tyrants that counts on our money, watching his country's beet crops grow whilst he runs out of bombs. 'Beet for bombs,' what could be better!"*

Laughter echoed around the room and the meeting ended on a high note that coincided with the ministerial bar opening.

Before departing, Eddie approached the foreign minister.

"Minister, I was hoping to discuss with you the possibility of a government grant to purchase the fifteen machines that I will need. The cloud machine owners that are subcontracted to work for me couldn't possibly afford the cost of the new model."

"No problem at all, Stormbart! With the advantage the government will get from this plan there will be no argument about providing you with the necessary funding."

Thinking of New Crews

With the delivery of the first new heavyweight cloud machine imminent, Eddie got down to planning his next weather convoy on behalf of the government. It would be little different from its predecessors other than the inclusion of the latest from deeper Salford. With a capacity equal to four of the current machines, there was no need to involve as many of the subcontracted machines as before, although the number could only be reduced by four.

Eddie drew up a list of forty-six crews to contact and that was a big enough job for a start but that was not all. He now had to find an additional two crew members to bring aboard his new model. He could ask one of the four crews that would not be travelling in their own machines but he was not particularly keen. Before he got further with the matter, Eddie's phone rang.

"Hello, Eddie, its Cirrus Cumulus here."

"Hello, Cirrus. What can I do for you?"

"Have you seen the article in today's Daily Gloom? I think it's all about the work you are doing for the government."

Eddie hadn't seen the newspaper and assured Cirrus he would take a look as soon as he could.

"While you are on, Cirrus, I wonder if you and Puffy would be interested in making up my crew numbers on the new machine. I need somebody I can depend on."

Whilst Cirrus was flattered, he had no desire to join in the routine associated with cloud convoys that could, from his own experience, last up to three weeks and more.

Picking up the Daily Gloom, Eddie couldn't miss the front page headline.

Beet the Bomb!
Government Reviews Foreign Aid

Reading on, the report made much of the government's intention of ensuring that, in future, any aid given to another country could only be used for what it was intended for. This was to be seen as a clampdown on those overseas tyrants that either enriched themselves from our monetary aid or used it to fund terrorism. In future it would deliver the rain that was so desperately needed for crop growing in drought-ridden countries. It would be a guarantee of beet instead of bombs. The report then went on to say how much the foreign aid budget could be reduced by and how the funding for weather delivery would provide employment in the UK.

Several ministers, along with the PM, were mentioned in the report in a prominent fashion but nowhere was there a mention of Eddie Stormbart and on that score he was not impressed, but neither was he surprised.

For the moment it was a case of reviewing who **'Stormbart's Weather Solutions'** had on its books and to organise the next convoy including an extra two crew members for the new machine.

A pamphlet was produced and sent out to every crew on the Stormbart's books explaining how things would be going forward over the next four years. No-one need fear of losing their contract with **'Stormbart's Weather Solutions'** and no-one would be required to dispose of their own machines. What was needed was for current crews to talk to each other and form up four-man crews to operate the new machines coming on line and they would be owned by the weather delivery company.

According to the pamphlet, everyone was a winner and the future looked bright, or at least wet, and that was a good thing. There was an excellent response to Eddie's master plan and within a short time he had the future crews he required and a few in reserve, and he drew up a calendar showing when each one would be married with a new machine. Now it was a case of waiting for the first of the new machines from Black, Black & Blackemore's.

Another conversation with Mr Spite drew Eddie's attention to the need for training. When all was said and done, he could hardly expect four crew members to simply jump aboard a brand new machine and operate it as if they had already been doing it for a lifetime. The pilot would not have anything new to learn about but the flight engineer would be faced with a much more complicated panel of dials and gauges to cope with and a greater workload. If anybody needed some training it would be the flight engineer. Eddie decided to discuss the best way forward with the manufacturers in deeper Salford.

It became patently obvious at an early stage of production that anyone piloting the machine would need to learn how it handles. Black, Black & Blackemore's test pilot, Johnny Black, together with test engineer, Ronnie Blackemore, both agreed that they should take the first machine to the Guild of Cloud Owners' training centre at Bishops Court in Northern Ireland to conduct flight testing and also to allow the training centre staff to develop a course around it. The training process was greatly aided by the production of a simulator which would allow any trainee crew to familiarise themselves with the layout and practice drills.

Everything was now in place and Eddie Stormbart looked forward excitedly to the arrival at Wythenshawe Weather Centre of the first of his new fleet of giant cloud machines. The whole of the weather-making world was looking forward to seeing Eddie's rain-making dream machine and everyone kept an eye open for an announcement of its launch date which was bound to be a big occasion.

The Launch

At Black, Black & Blackemore's factory in deeper Salford, the first new double-decker cloud machine was eventually rolled out and test pilot, Johnny Black, and test engineer, Ronnie Blackemore, flew it to Bishops Court to begin testing. The test programme went like a song and it wasn't long before they felt they could make a delivery flight to Wythenshawe, but that would have to wait for the training staff to design a training programme.

When Mr Spite was aware of the delivery date of the new machine he had to act quickly to organise things, or at least his secretary, Goldilocks, did. It wasn't long before the official launch details appeared in the Monthly Downpour and the subject became the talking point amongst everyone associated with weather delivery.

Wythenshawe's huge hangar was emptied of all its resident cloud machines and thoroughly cleaned before being given a fresh coat of paint both inside and out. A position in the centre of the hangar was marked out as the place the new machine would occupy on the big day. On each side of the machine, that is to say, on its port and starboard sides, tiers of seating were erected for the expected throng. A raised platform was placed adjacent to the position of the nose of the craft to allow the process of naming to be carried out by some dignitary. There was also a stage to accommodate a prominent Band that would be brought in specially.

Once the launch date had appeared in the Monthly Downpour there was a rush to get tickets and, for once, Goldilocks got flustered by all the demands being made upon her, but that's not really surprising. Some of the demands were not for tickets for the launching. Some were rather appealing, she thought, but she did resist temptation in the end, even though it was frustrating saying no!

Johnny Black and Ronnie Blackemore brought the new machine to Wythenshawe from Northern Ireland on a very dark night. Only a skeleton crew was around to witness its arrival. It landed on the concrete apron in front of the huge hangar and, once alighted, its fan duct motors were shut down. A tractor arrived to push the machine, stern first, into the darkened hangar. It was a delicate operation to manoeuvre it into its precisely designated position but once the hangar doors were shut, the lights came on and the job got much easier.

People from the weather world started to arrive in droves the following mid-morning and entered the huge hangar to take their seats. The new machine looked grand, all polished and shiny, but what was most imposing about it was its double-decker look. It had the same length and width as the machines currently operating from Wythenshawe but it was twice as tall. Its setting in the super clean, freshly painted hangar was magnificent and Wingates Band added to it with their splendid music that sounded so regal. Their blue jackets and white roses for button-holes together with their shiny brass instruments added to the scene.

"I don't think it was a good idea to launch this machine on Friday the thirteenth. What do you think, Cirrus?"

"It's Captain Cumulus to you, Puffy. Just remember that. I am inclined to agree with you, however. Friday the thirteenth can be unlucky."

"You're right there, skipper," replied Puffy.

Whenever there is a gathering of cloud machine owners and their crews it is inevitable that conversations strike up and greetings are in abundance. Many of those present saw little of their colleagues during most of the year. Clearly, once this launch was out of the way, the Silver Lining Club was going to do good business, but for the moment, Wythenshawe's huge hangar was filled with a cacophony of sound provided by a mixture of music and a talking throng.

At the appointed time, the music stopped and the Centre's Superintendent, Mr I.N.Spite CDM, stepped onto the raised platform aside the nose of the new craft. The talking stopped for here was a person held in high esteem by all that knew him.

"Ladies, gentlemen, fellow weather-makers, we are gathered here today to witness the launching of a very special new cloud machine, and to perform the launching I am to extend on your behalf a greeting to our foreign minister, the right honourable Douglas Mackintosh."

There then followed an applause which was a mixture of hand-clapping, booing and raspberry-blowing but it was all foreign to the right honourable Douglas Mackintosh who was more interested in the magnum of champagne placed on the table in front of him. His interest was noted by Eddie Stormbart who was also present and cautiously he whispered in the foreign minister's ear, *"Don't you dare dent my new machine with that bottle or you will have me to answer to."*

The right honourable Douglas Mackintosh turned to face those seated behind the platform leaving his back to those seated on the other side of the new machine, but they didn't mind.

"We are all gathered here today to witness the launching of the government's new foreign aid policy."

That foxed a fair number of those gathered who thought they had come to witness the launching of a new model of cloud machine and they started to think about making an early departure for The Silver Lining Club. Before they could put their coats back on, the minister continued.

"Very soon, you will all be taking vast quantities of government rain to the four corners of the world to help those most in need of it."

There then followed a twenty minute party political speech and the audience only awoke when Wingates Band's fanfare of cornets livened the proceedings.

The right honourable Douglas Mackintosh grabbed hold of a cord that was attached to a sash that was covering up the name of the new machine and began to speak again.

*"I name this cloud machine **Cloudtanic** and good luck to all who rain in her."*

The cord was pulled to reveal the name on the side of the machine. The Band struck up and the audience stood and cheered and hats were thrown in the air to find new owners.

The various dignitaries stepped down off the platform which was then moved to allow the ***Cloudtanic*** to be towed by a tractor toward the hangar's opening doors. In the sunshine outdoors the newly named machine sparkled and the media got their first look. There would be a lot of front page photos next day but for those that had come to witness the launching the show was over and they headed for a reunion in the Silver Lining Club.

The foreign minister and his political colleagues sat around a table with a magnum of champagne, toasting their own intellectual wisdom, whilst those who had made it all possible, Eddie Stormbart, the design team from deeper Salford, the company test crew and Wythenshawe's Superintendent sat drinking at another and watched with incredulity.

A maiden voyage

It was time now for Eddie to think about forming a crew for the *Cloudtanic*. His own machine, the *Waterwonder* would be mothballed in Wythenshawe's huge hangar and he and his Flight Engineer, Fred Fuller, would switch to the new machine but he still required another two crew members. After some deliberation he offered the job to the crew of the *Raindrop* and they accepted.

Pilot, Andy McNabb, and flight engineer, Matt Summers, were only too pleased to be forming a crew with Eddie Stormbart aboard the *Cloudtanic*. The experience would look good on their CV and it should assist them gaining work in the future. They were also committed to the notion that the weather business needed to get bigger to get better, although that really depended on whether you were delivering rain or on the receiving end of it.

With the *Waterwonder* and *Raindrop* mothballed, the four intrepid cloud fliers departed for Bishops Court Training Centre where they would be introduced to the *Cloudtanic* and learn how to fly it and take advantage of its weather-making capacity.

Within a relatively short time, the new crew was deemed proficient and was awarded a licence to operate the latest piece of technology from deeper Salford. It was now time to consolidate the training by performing a maiden voyage to fully test its capabilities. Once that was done, Eddie could get back to weather convoys for the government.

Manchester is a city with a proud tradition of dark skies, wind and rain. Its true claim to fame in recent times were the world famous Manchester Blacks, a cloud of true distinction that looked ferocious and which produced prolific rainfalls the drops of which could bounce to incredible heights upon hitting the ground. These clouds were the scourge of any skirt-wearing lady and even the hardy kilt-wearing Scotsman would think twice about venturing out when a Manchester Black had been spotted. Manchester's weather had been the making of those hardy northerners who had gone on to make their mark on the world. Manchester's weather was something to boast about and as luck would have it an important date loomed.

July 15th may not be important to many folks but in Manchester, the opposite was true. Being St.Swithin's Day it was folklore that if it rained on this day, it would rain for the next forty days and nights. It was considered important to maintain this tradition, but of course some of the less hardy souls preferred that it didn't rain at all on July 15th but they were about to run out of luck.

At Bishops Court Training Centre the *Cloudtanic* was provisioned for a task of considerable duration and Eddie Stormbart ensured that he had lots of CDs of his favourite Brass Band which was celebrating its 140th anniversary this year. Eddie was particularly proud that he had been made a trustee of his beloved Wingates Band and he didn't want to lose touch with them on a long job. As soon as it became dark, the *Cloudtanic* emerged from the Centre's hangar and ascended into the night sky. A course was set for Liverpool Bay but the machine was eventually brought to a hover east of the Isle-of-Man. Eddie and his flight engineer, Fred, were doing the first shift and it fell to Fred to perform the first atomisation of water on a real job. To atomise 16,000,000 gallons of North Sea took some time but at the end of it a large Manchester Black had been created around the *Cloudtanic* and every water storage tank and refrigerator on board was full. Now it was time to deliver, and maintain an important tradition.

The Manchester Black was soon on the move and it crept slowly towards that great northern city. Leeds had vied for the privilege but if you are delivering Manchester Blacks, then there is only one city that is appropriate to be on the receiving end. Timing was critical. It was important not to arrive before the 15th. The airspeed had to be adjusted several times to ensure that the *Cloudtanic* did not get into position too early but it was done with great precision.

The darkness of night gave way in Manchester to the shadow of a Manchester Black and there was not much difference. Early morning risers setting out for work knew instinctively that they were going to get it, they just didn't know exactly when. The population of the city was getting about with a hurried purpose and not without casting a regular eye on what was above. Those that had accomplished the skill of early morning talking remarked on the quality of the cloud job above and fresh enquiries began about the whereabouts of St.Swithin and what he should do with his Manchester Blacks. It was just as well that Eddie Stormbart and his three colleagues couldn't hear what was being said by those city folk they were currently hovering above.

For the next forty days and forty nights, the *Cloudtanic* remained above a very wet Manchester. The great city got rained on with a regularity that befits the tradition. It wasn't constant rain but it was very wet rain and it did prove how effective the new machine from deeper Salford was.

For forty days and forty nights Manchester was a city of *uproar* and *downpour* but the hardy northerners survived and the art of constructing Arks made a remarkable comeback. More important than all of this, however, was the fact that the *Cloudtanic* had proved itself and it was time now to get on with the work it had been designed for. Government work lay ahead.

AMOROUS TIMES

Gardening was a job that Puffy enjoyed and at the Slaidburn home that he shared with his skipper, Cirrus Cumulus, there was always something that needed his attention. Gardening was always an opportunity to chew over issues that affected him and, currently, the burning one was the new female in his life, Goldilocks.

For some time, Puffy had wanted to invite his current idol to Slaidburn. He was sure that it would make a good impression on her and more to the point, it would be a chance to test out her wrestling skills on home ground. The problem was Cirrus! His skipper had strict views about married men cavorting with young single females. Cirrus tended to be quite straight-laced about some things and he would have to be very diplomatic if he was going to get him to agree to Goldilocks coming to stay.

Mowing the lawn, hoeing the borders and clearing the weeds made the garden look nice but it didn't provide the inspiration that Puffy was looking for. He went over his circumstances time after time to try and realise a plan but it was all to no avail. The situation was really quite straightforward, he thought. He had married Carol Aspinall on the spur of the moment and, for the short time they were together, everything had been fine. It was the prospect of the pair of them having to live in a caravan, albeit temporarily, that proved too much for her and she upped and left him.

He occasionally saw Carol at Wythenshawe Weather Centre but there was no rapport between them. To all intents and purposes, they were married now in name only, and that was that. Puffy considered himself to be a free agent when it came to women but he still had to convince his skipper.

When the gardening was done, Puffy still had no idea how to approach Cirrus and, consequently, he decided to put the issue of inviting Goldilocks over onto the back burner. He knew from experience that if he didn't think things through before approaching his skipper, he would be doomed to failure. For the moment he would wait until something opportune arose and with that he retired to the kitchen to make a coffee.

The Daily Gloom had an amazing impact on Captain Cirrus Cumulus, who read some of its contents with great interest. Issues affecting how the UK was governed had a special place in the mind of Cirrus, although he was in no way active politically. He was an armchair politician in current despair, and he shared it with his flight engineer, whether he liked it or not. No more than ten percent of the newspaper interested Cirrus and, strangely, it was his star prediction that ran a close second to politics but he did not necessarily share his horoscope with Puffy. It was always wise to try and work out the best time to walk in on Cirrus when he had his head in the Daily Gloom and a withdrawal strategy could be helpful.

The coffee was made and the bacon was almost cooked and it smelled good. Puffy took a quick look at Cirrus through the partly opened lounge door. It was impossible to judge his skipper's temperament since his head was buried in the newspaper. Returning to the kitchen, Puffy finished the mid-morning refreshments and took them on a tray into the lounge.

"Ah, there you are, Puffy. The bacon smells good!"

That was a good omen, thought Puffy, but omens often proved to be wrong and this was going to be one of those occasions.

"You know, I feel desperately sad that the Scottish Parliament want to go independent."

Puffy hadn't seen this one coming. He hadn't taken a quick look at the newspaper this morning and he knew he was going to pay the price.

"The Scottish Parliament think that the UK government have been creaming off all the North Sea oil revenue. They think they have been short-changed. They have this idea that if they had independence they could spend the oil revenue on Scotland and be much better off. What happens when the oil runs out? That's what I want to know."

There was a short pause whilst Cirrus took a bite out of his bacon butty, but it didn't last.

"These Scottish MPs make it all sound so simple but I'm not sure that it is. There are a lot of companies that operate both in England and Scotland, how will they be affected? What about law and order, health and education, how will they be affected? What about all the treaties that we are currently signed up to? Will an independent Scotland have to re-negotiate all of them?"

Clearly, Cirrus felt very strongly about this issue and it was not going to be over in a few minutes. He returned to the subject of Scottish devolution with a vengeance.

"There are questions about currency and sovereignty and membership of the European Union. There are a vast number of issues. These politician Wallers are mad to try and convince anyone that it will be simple to do."

Whilst he may have started as a passive listener, Puffy was roused by the issue that his skipper had raised and it got him thinking.

"I think you are right, skipper, and it begs the question about water and energy supplies. Don't we get a lot of that from Scotland and vice versa?"

Cirrus looked at his flight engineer slightly disbelieving but had to admit to himself that he had a point.

"You know, one of the things that will be a big problem is defence. For a start, we are only just bringing back our troops from Germany and some of them are going to Scotland. The army, navy and air force have important bases in Scotland. What's going to happen to them? The Scottish MPs say they will have their own army. It all sounds completely mad and it's bound to cost a phenomenal amount of money and just at a time when we don't have it. Who's going to protect Scottish airspace and Scottish waters?"

This was all very interesting, but Puffy had a desire to move onto something else and preferably away from his skipper who was getting too engrossed in something he had no control over.

"I hate to think of the break-up of the United Kingdom. Scotland with all its rich traditions is a vital part of our culture. I love the Scots and all that they bring to our island nation. You know, Puffy, it seems mad that at a time when the EU is trying to drag us all into one large European Nation that Scotland wants to break away from the UK to form an independent country. It's diametrically opposite to what else is happening."

Puffy didn't have a clue what that meant but conceded that it sounded good.

"I'm greatly disappointed with our political masters and the situations they are getting us into."

That was the last uttering's on the subject by Cirrus, who slumped dejectedly into his chair staring into nowhere. It was time for Puffy to make his tactful withdrawal, and he did.

An Invitation

A knock on the front door announced the arrival of the postman.

"Aurora Cloudealis! That's a funny name for a house," remarked the postman as he handed a wad of letters to Puffy.

The postman wouldn't have time to listen to the story as to how the house had acquired the name and Puffy had no inclination to tell it.

"Its original though isn't it," he remarked to the postman who was already departing to complete his round of deliveries.

"Anything interesting arrived, Puffy?" enquired Cirrus.

The wad of letters was handed to his skipper and he left him to wade through them. A few minutes passed before Cirrus announced that he'd better return. Something of interest had arrived.

Eddie Stormbart was a fanatical Brass Band supporter and as a trustee of the famous Wingates Band he had a vested interest in celebrating its 140th anniversary. The Band was putting on a celebratory concert at Bolton's Victoria Hall, a very special place in the Band's long history. The Band's composer in residence, Lucy Pankhurst, had composed two special pieces of music which would be premiered at the concert and Eddie was most excited about the prospect.

"Puffy, we have just received an invitation to a great celebration in Bolton."

"Who's that from, skipper?"

"It's from Eddie Stormbart."

"And what's the celebration about?"

"It's the 140th anniversary of Wingates Band and Eddie has sent us four tickets."

"That was music to Puffy's ears. This was the opportunity he had been waiting for.

"Who are you going to take, skipper?"

"You know the answer to that. If Abigail is free, I'm going to take her. What about you?"

"Well I can't take the missus since she's left and I wouldn't want to let Eddie down, so I think I'll ask Goldilocks."

There was a pause in the conversation but after a few moments and much to the relief of Puffy, Cirrus suggested they'd better get in contact with the two ladies.

Cirrus and Puffy didn't have long to wait in front of Bolton's imposing Town Hall on the night of the concert. First to arrive was Abigail who looked as attractive as ever. She was not a flamboyant dresser but she didn't need to be. Her tall slim figure allowed her to carry off almost any form of dress wear and the sight of her this Saturday evening melted Cirrus. The same could also be said about the way Goldilocks looked. Her taste in dress was very unlike that of Carol but for the moment, the least said about that the better, thought Puffy.

The two couples greeted each other with enthusiasm before linking arms and strolling down Bolton's Knowsley Street to the Victoria Hall and they swaggered a little as they did so. As they all entered the hall they were greeted by Eddie.

"Nice to see you all here tonight! I do hope you will enjoy the concert."

"I'm sure that we will, and thank you, Eddie, for the invitation," replied Cirrus.

"And ladies! How attractive you both look tonight," commented Eddie.

It was too difficult to tell who was most pleased by this comment, the men or the women, but it was most gratifying to hear.

After a little small talk, the two couples purchased concert programmes before making their way into the main hall and finding themselves a suitable place to sit.

The programme looked good and certainly the two men, and possibly Abigail, could anticipate some enjoyable numbers, but Goldilocks was less knowledgeable about the world of Brass although she was caught up in the atmosphere. The hall steadily filled with enthusiasts and when it was full it looked most impressive. The talking point was, of course, the 140 years of a band that had started life as one of Britain's temperance bands and had gone on to claim a place in history with some of its contesting achievements. To have survived without a break and through two world wars was certainly something to talk about and the audience hummed with anecdotes from the past.

"They were a reet champion band when that chap William Rimmer wert conductor."

"Ah but that were around 1903/1904 when they did the double, double."

Folks in this part of the world knew a thing or two about Wingate's Band and stories from past and present abounded until the Band's President and

MC for the night, Dr David Kaye, stepped proudly onto Victoria Hall's stage to welcome everyone.

With introductions and welcomes out of the way, it was time for the Band to make its entry on stage and as it did so the audience stood to greet it. It was splendid to see the resplendent band players in their blue and gold laced uniforms strut onto the stage, each holding a highly polished instrument. Cornets, horns, euphoniums, baritones, trombones and those huge tubas were all there and the percussionists took up their positions at the back of the stage.

There is nothing to compare with the resounding start of a Brass Band concert and in true tradition this occasion was no different. The audience was wooed by the collection of pieces played in the first half of the concert and heartily gave an appreciative applause after each one. Wingate's Band may have been around for 140 years but judging by the quality of its current music making, it would be around for a lot longer.

At the interval Cirrus, Abigail, Puffy and Goldilocks made their way to the refreshments area. They were all enjoying the concert immensely and Goldilocks had been surprised by the whole experience. She had never been to this type of concert before and was unsure what to expect but she had not been disappointed. The whole evening was proving to be a great experience.

Whilst the four concert goers enjoyed a coffee, Puffy spied out of the corner of his eye a certain lady by the name of Carol White, formerly Aspinall, making her way towards him. He had been facing one kind of music in the hall but it looked as if he was about to face another kind here. There was no opportunity to warn any of the others or to take cover. He would just have to face the music coming to him and it would probably not be pleasant on the ears.

"So this is what you get up to when I'm not around!" said Carol as an opening barrage.

"You left me didn't you so what's the gripe?" replied Puffy.

"I'm still your wife don't forget, and who's this trollop you've got on your arm?"

Those standing around couldn't help overhear the conversation which now had the makings of a drama and an audience to watch it play out.

Goldilocks was most upset both at being called a trollop and at discovering that Puffy was married. Events had suddenly taken a nasty turn.

Cirrus and Abigail took the initiative and led Goldilocks, who was clearly upset, back into the hall and left Puffy to remonstrate with Carol.

There was not much remonstrating to do. Carol had left Puffy some time ago, so why should she be bothered that he had someone else on his arm? Was she jealous?

When challenged, she denied it and stormed off with the words, *"I couldn't care less who you are sleeping with!"*

Watching Carol depart in her multi-coloured outfit, Puffy couldn't help feeling totally confused by her actions as did the throng that had witnessed the incident, but now it was time to get back to Goldilocks and see how she was.

The second half of the concert was performed in great style by Wingate's Band but the enjoyment had gone right out of it for Goldilocks and Puffy and the end couldn't come too soon for them. After a wonderful finale, a proud Dr David Kaye stepped onto the stage to congratulate the Band on a sterling performance. He then went on to thank everybody for attending and wish them a safe journey home and sealed the end by saying that he hoped he would see them all again in another 140 years time.

"It will probably be at a different venue," quipped someone and a huge laugh accompanied it.

Puffy was hoping that as he left the hall there would not be a second encounter with his estranged wife and he was lucky. He spotted her leaving and she was arm in arm with another bloke that he didn't recognise.

Well that beats everything, thought Puffy, but his attention now was to placate his date for the night, Goldilocks. She had clearly been upset by the earlier fracas.

The plan had been to invite the two ladies back to Slaidburn for the night but that didn't look likely now.

"Puffy, I think I would like to go home now," said Goldilocks.

"Will I be able to see you again?" enquired Puffy.

"I don't think that will be a good idea. I didn't realise you were still married and I think you need to sort that before dating anyone again."

Puffy was despondent at this point but had a feeling that this would be the outcome and felt obliged to agree. He apologised to Goldilocks for the situation she had had to endure but thanked her for coming and they parted their ways.

It was obvious to both Cirrus and Abigail that there would not be the best of atmospheres in Slaidburn at the present moment and they decided to go their separate ways for the time being. Whilst this was most disappointing to the pair of them, they both felt for Puffy and his needs right now were greater than theirs.

A New Venture

Cirrus had developed a fascination with the current idea being exploited by Eddie Stormbart. His latest cloud machine, the *Cloudtanic* had a lot of potential. For a start, thought Cirrus, he could do several jobs with only one atomisation process required, and that would not only save time but also make jobs more profitable. Being able to convey some 16,000,000 gallons of water in a combination of cloud vapour, ice and water was mind-boggling. The thought of cutting out three out of every four flights from Wythenshawe Weather Centre to the Irish Sea to atomise brine sounded very appealing. It would not be so effective if the rain he had to deliver was of a specified variety. On the other hand, using a particular quality of rainwater was a fairly rare thing these days. The equipment on board most machines tended to create rain of a reasonably consistent grading, irrespective of the source. In spite of all that, there would still be a requirement in the future for rain using a specific grade of water.

A cloud machine like the *Cloudtanic* had a lot going for it, thought Cirrus, but the cost of purchasing one could be astronomical and given that he had only recently purchased the latest model from Black, Black & Blackemore's, a Star AW Mk1, it was not likely to be a feasible possibility. Even so, he was reluctant not to explore the idea further and he decided to discuss it with his Flight Engineer.

After considerable debate, it was concluded that a possible way forward would be to sign up as a crew with Eddie Stormbart's organisation – 'Stormbart's Weather Solutions' and gain some experience of operating one of his new cloud craft. Cirrus was extremely loath to do this since he still felt that the convoy work that Eddie was involved with was too routine and awfully boring. He had to concede however that this may be the only chance he may have to fly one. If he was lucky, he might get an opportunity of using one of Eddie's craft for a job of his own between cloud convoys, but that was a bit of a long shot.

"Hello, Eddie, its Cirrus Cumulus here."

"Hello, Cirrus, what can I do for you?"

"Eddie, are you still in need of crews for your new machines?"

"Yes I am but don't tell me that you are interested! I thought you had plenty work to keep you going with your own machine."

"That's true, I do Eddie, but to tell you the truth, I would like to gain some experience operating one of the giant jobs that you will be using on your convoys."

"Don't tell me you are thinking of getting one?"

"I might. From what knowledge I have, I would say it has a lot going for it."

"I would be happy to sign you up, Cirrus, but I think you will soon get fed up with the routine of Convoy work; I know you only too well. Anyway, you will only be one half of a crew."

"What do you mean by that?"

"The Cloudtanic requires a four man crew."

There was a pause as Cirrus took this information in.

"Have you got a four man crew, Cirrus?"

This was clearly a stumbling block. Cirrus had not taken this into consideration.

"No I haven't. I'm going to have to sort that."

"Well you do that, Cirrus, and then get back to me."

The thought of finding another pilot and another flight engineer to team up with seemed daunting to begin with but then Cirrus began thinking about Abigail. This could be an opportunity to spend more time with her, although a working environment was not exactly romantic but it was practical.

"Puffy, if I want to sign on with Eddie I will have to find another pilot and flight engineer to join us. I was thinking of asking Abigail to join us. How would you feel about that?"

"I don't mind that at all skipper. Give Abigail a ring and see what she has to say."

"I will need to find a flight engineer as well," added Cirrus.

Puffy was a bit despondent at this point. If things had been different he could have had a female companion to assist him, but alas, that was not the case.

A few days later, Cirrus got round to giving Abigail a call. He discussed the possibility of her joining his crew on one of Eddie Stormbart's new giant cloud machines and she jumped at the idea. She had already done a lot of work for Eddie and didn't mind the routine associated with his work at all. She also suggested that her flight engineer, Josh Harrop, might be prepared to join them. Whilst making this suggestion she was acutely aware that Puffy may have preferred another female crew member and as a result, Josh might have to be left on the shelf.

"I think we need to include Josh if we are going to be able to sign up. I don't think there is much chance of Puffy finding a flight engineer companion at present. He will just have to put up with Josh," remarked Cirrus.

"In that case, I will have a word with Josh and let you know."

For the moment, that's where matters were left.

A week passed and the subject of Stormbart's Weather Solutions was never touched on. Puffy had been away for a couple of days and his return was eagerly awaited by Cirrus. Microwave cooking was not a patch on Puffy's gastronomical wonders and having to interrupt newspaper reading sessions with coffee-making rankled him. Puffy had a role in the life of Cirrus and he liked it.

Puffy's car drew up outside the front door of the Slaidburn home he shared with his skipper. He opened the front door and stepped into the lounge to face Cirrus.

Cirrus was enormously pleased to see him.

"Skipper, I have a flight engineer to join us."

Cirrus looked at him in startled amazement.

"Come in!" shouted Puffy.

Through the lounge door came a female dressed in the most outrageous and gregarious of clothes, yellow tights, a blue top and green scarf.

"The wife's back!" announced Puffy.

FROM CLOUDTANIC A GONDALUS IS BORN

T he post dropped through the letter-box of the Slaidburn home of Cirrus Cumulus and his faithful engineer, Puffy, picked it up and took it through to the lounge along with a cup of coffee.

"Did I hear the post arrive, Puffy?"

"You did indeed, Captain, and here it is along with your morning coffee."

"Good man, Puffy. What would I ever do without you?"

Perhaps that last comment was aimed at the fact that Carol was back on the scene and she may want to introduce some different living arrangements. For the moment he would let sleeping dogs lie, he thought.

Cirrus looked through the small collection of differently sized envelopes to see if anything looked interesting. As usual, the majority of the post was from a range of different companies trying to sell stuff and that was immediately confined to his rubbish basket. There wasn't much left after that. The envelope with the 'Guild of Cloud Owners' on the back was probably the latest edition of the Monthly Downpour. He opened it to find that he had guessed correctly.

Generally, there was always one article in the journal that was of interest to him and this edition was no different. Looking at the contents page, Cirrus noticed an article on new EU regulations about to come into force. Before he even found the page on which the article appeared, his blood pressure started to rise. He could be confident that whatever the EU was about to impose on the country, it would not be to its advantage. Given that an article was appearing in the Monthly Downpour, he assumed it was to do with the business he was involved in, making rain and other things!

Puffy was about to enter the lounge to collect Cirrus' coffee cup but upon hearing his ranting and raving, he decided to postpone his waiter service and retired to the kitchen.

Cirrus knew that the European Union had been considering passing regulations on weather-making since the 'Guild of Cloud Owners' had held a meeting at Wythenshawe Weather Centre to discuss the issue. A deputation had gone to Brussels to ensure that the views of the Guild's members were made known. At the time, it was a bit of a fiasco since the assembly had done one of its moves to Strasbourg and the Brussels office was empty. Eventually, an exasperated Guild President, Mr George Fowlup CDM, did manage to track down the relevant people and made the Guild's views very clear. All that was some time ago.

Although Cirrus was very frustrated by the new EU regulations he had to concede that the Guild had been very effective in staving off a raft of ideas that were just plain daft.

Studying the article carefully, he could see that the proposal to ban cloud machines from raining on Sundays had been scrapped. It had made no practical sense since nature does it anyway and although the EU would have liked to have imposed its regulation on nature, it didn't know where its head office was. The same thing had also applied to the proposed regulation to impose a speed limit on cloud machines. The EU was aware that it had no jurisdiction over nature's wind but also that the 'Guild of Cloud Owners' self-regulated this matter already.

Reading further, Cirrus discovered that other proposals had been quashed; confining thunder and lightning to rural areas had met with considerable opposition from farmers, particularly in France. The imposition of parking fees or hovering fees had been considered impractical. Much of this was down to nature and members of the European Parliament had felt particularly frustrated that their jurisdiction had not yet embraced it.

Another two proposals had been thrown out, both reluctantly. Banning cloud machines from flying in the opposite direction to nature's stuff whilst visible to the public had merit but it was already regulated by the Guild, not to mention that on occasion it was essential to allow it. National emergencies of one form or another may in fact, demand it, fire-fighting being one of them. The topping up of lakes and reservoirs using matching water also had merit but once more this was already self- regulated by the 'Guild of Cloud Owners'.

The Guild had clearly been most effective in putting to a stop much of the intended interference by the EU but it had not stopped all regulation. The most threatening piece of legislation related to the amount of water that a cloud machine was allowed to atomise. The original proposal had been to limit each machine to 2,000,000 gallons per month. This would have decimated the small industry. In fact, the industry would have disappeared if this regulation had been passed. After much debate in twenty-six countries, twenty-five of whom have no part in the industry, a very much watered- down regulation was passed for enforcement. From now on, the EU decreed that all cloud machines be confined to atomising a maximum of 4,000,000 gallons of water but there was no limit imposed on how many times they could do this per month. In order to monitor this, another regulation had been passed imposing on each cloud owner the requirement to have a *'tachogallon'* installed which would be inspected each time a machine undergoes an MOT test.

Cirrus called out for Puffy to join him and to bring another coffee and he discussed the EU rules with him.

"On the whole, Puffy, it looks like we have got off pretty lightly. From what I can make of it, we can carry on the same as before. The only difference it makes to us is that we will have to have a tachogallon installed on the Nimbus."

Puffy was most pleased that his skipper had calmed down and was viewing things in such a rational way. It made a change from the way he normally reacted to all things EU.

"Yes you're right, skipper. I have to give credit to the Guild and to its President, George Fowlup in particular. They have done a pretty good job."

The crew of the Nimbus paused and drank coffee before speaking again.

"There is one person that will be badly affected by these regulations."

"You mean Eddie Stormbart, skipper."

"That's exactly who I mean. His new machine, the Cloudtanic, can't operate under these new rules."

"I wonder if he's seen the article?" enquired Puffy, who then made a discreet withdrawal as he noticed his Captain dropping into a deep bout of thinking.

Several hours later, the phone rang and Puffy picked it up.

"Hello, Mr Stormbart. What can I do for you?"

Eddie wanted to speak to Cirrus and the call was put through to him in the lounge.

"Good morning, Eddie."

"There's not much good about it," began Eddie. *"I suppose you have read the latest edition of the Monthly Downpour?"*

"Yes I have, Eddie, and I suppose it's the article on the new EU rules that you are calling about?"

"Cirrus, that new regulation limiting us to 4,000,000 gallons spells the end of the Cloudtanic!"

Cirrus could tell how upset Eddie was by the tone of his voice.

"I thought the new rule only limited us to atomising 4,000,000 gallons at a time. There was no limit on how many times you could do it, or any time limit between carrying out atomising. Surely you can do four separate sessions in a day and still top up to 16,000,000 gallons."

"Don't be daft, Cirrus! If that was the case there would be no point to the regulation at all. If you look at the small print you would see that no cloud machine will be able to move more than 4,000,000 gallons at any one time."

Cirrus felt a bit stupid after Eddie's last comment since it should have been pretty obvious as to what the rule meant. It had been one of those cases of 'engaging mouth before brain'.

"I take your point, Eddie."

"What the devil am I going to do now with the Cloudtanic? There is no longer a purpose for it."

"I suggest you get on to the government. It's the government that got us into the EU. Let them sort it out, and let them sort it out with Black, Black & Blackemore's."

With that, Eddie made some kind of a grunt and the phone went dead.

Puffy joined Cirrus in the lounge and the pair of them discussed Eddie's plight. Neither of them could think of a way round the problem other than Eddie moving his operation to somewhere outside the EU's jurisdiction but that was fraught with difficulties. For a start, it would not look good for the government to be seen attempting to circumvent EU rules when it was a member of the EU itself. Secondly, even if it did this, many of the cloud machine owners contracted to Eddie had their machines registered in the UK. It was all rather complicated and if it became a legal matter it would cost a fortune. They both agreed that Eddie was faced with a conundrum.

A Germ of an Idea

A couple of days later, Cirrus was listening to the radio and an interview was taking place with a young lady called Molly Schofield. Cirrus thought he recognised the name but for the moment he couldn't remember from where. Molly was asked by her interviewer to describe for the listeners how she had once been jilted by her boyfriend and had gained revenge on him. Her story was most unusual and it triggered Cirrus' memory. Evidently, Molly's boyfriend had been two-timing her and what made it worse, he had been doing it with her best friend.

Listeners could sympathise with Molly. She had been cruelly deceived. What listeners were not prepared for was Molly's remarkable story of how she got her own back. She described how she had read an advert in the local press which had read:

Hire a Downpour
Got a grudge? Got a score to settle? Want to get your own back?
Ever considered drenching someone or a crowd?
Why not consider hiring a downpour!
It's not illegal, and no-one gets hurt, just wet.

This had set Molly's mind working and she not only hired a downpour, she also got a ride on the cloud delivering it. She then went on to describe how the downpour was delivered as her previous friends were posing for their wedding photographs outside a church in Clitheroe. She deliberately left out the bit about the rain being green and how it had stained all of the wedding party's clothes. She thought that that might cast her in a bad light.

The radio interview was followed by a large number of phone calls to the programme and a good proportion was asking for details of how to contact the service Molly had used. Judging by the response, there were a lot of females out there who felt just like Molly had.

Whilst the interview had been entertaining to listen to, it had got Cirrus seriously thinking. He clearly remembered the wedding in Clitheroe but, more importantly, he also remembered how a number of people had been prepared to pay for the experience of flying in a cloud machine. Perhaps there could be something in this, thought Cirrus.

Puffy was called to join Cirrus in the lounge and for protection he brought coffee and a bacon butty. He knew that Cirrus loved this mid morning.

"Ah, that's great, Puffy. You know me too well. Anyway I want to share an idea with you."

I wonder what he wants me to do this time, thought Puffy.

Cirrus went on to talk about the radio interview he had just been listening to.

"Oh I remember Molly Schofield. She had a lovely figure."

"Never mind that," interjected Cirrus who went on, *"She was just one of a number of people who paid to fly with us."*

Puffy could only remember two but allowed his Captain to exaggerate without interrupting.

"I've been thinking! I think that if we offered people a chance to do a cruise with us they would jump at the chance."

"What are you on about, skipper? There's no room on the Nimbus to carry passengers."

"I'm not talking about the Nimbus; I'm talking about the Cloudtanic. Suppose that the upper deck was converted into grand accommodation for a fee paying couple and we offered them a cruise like they do on those cruise liners."

This got Puffy thinking too. Maybe this was an idea worth exploiting.

"Just think of it, Puffy, we could offer to exchange air waves for sea waves."

The discussion then moved on to how the top deck of the Cloudtanic would need to be altered to provide suitable accommodation. Since there was no longer a need for all the extra water storage tanks and refrigerators, they could be removed to make way for a bedroom, toilet, bathroom, lounge and dining area. The details were sketched in a notepad.

"We would need to take a chef with us to cater for passengers with taste," remarked Puffy.

"I agree, and we would still require a crew of four to man it if we are going to cruise for several weeks," added Cirrus.

"There wouldn't be much for any passenger to see if they spent all their time on the top deck, skipper."

"You're right but if we put a TV screen up there coupled to the TV camera then they will see what we see and we could also install a PPI (Plan Position Indicator) for them so that they could keep track of where they are."

After the initial flurry of enthusiasm, Puffy was becoming more sceptical about the idea. Living on the top deck of the Cloudtanic for a few weeks with no company and only a TV screen and a PPI to view the outside world didn't sound so exciting and he told Cirrus so. Cirrus accused him of lacking imagination.

"Look, Puffy, what we do on a cruise is plan an itinerary which includes us stopping every night at a fresh venue so that the passengers can go ashore, so to speak.

"And how do you propose that we get them ashore?"

"Puffy, you really are hard work! If we plan that each place we visit is a coastal resort then we descend to sea level and get a boat to come out and collect the passengers."

"What if it's not a coastal resort?"

"Well in that case we just get a guide to walk through our cloud to meet and greet our passengers and then escort them to wherever they want to go."

That was as far as things could be taken at this point but the pair of them agreed that the idea was worth exploring further with Eddie, and with that the discussion ended and as it did so, rain began to fall on the lounge window.

"I wonder if that's nature's stuff or one of ours," remarked Cirrus.

Things Move Forward

Eddie Stormbart thought the idea of cloud cruise holidays had a lot of merit and when the government conceded defeat, once again, to the new almighty power of Brussels, its merit increased dramatically. Government plans to change foreign aid from money to rain, using the Cloudtanic, was now an acute embarrassment to it. It now had the cost of this new machine to absorb, as well as the rest that it had ordered, to add to its burden. For those who follow these things, which included Cirrus Cumulus, there was nothing new about this kind of government fiasco. Eddie decided to drop in on his friend Cirrus and explore matters further.

"I think you have something with this cloud cruise holiday idea, Cirrus, but let's have a look at the changes to the design of the Cloudtanic."

The two men pored over the sketches that Cirrus had made with the aid of his flight engineer.

"I'd say these look pretty good, Cirrus, but we need to take them to Black, Black & Blackemore's and see what they have to say."

What about the government, Eddie? They own the Cloudtanic; will they not want a stake in the idea?"

"Not on your life, Cirrus. The government has enough EU egg on its face right now. If you made them an offer for the Cloudtanic, you would probably get it for a song. The government's interest in cloud machines is at an all time low. They currently have this machine on their hands and don't know what to do with it."

Cirrus had not really thought about buying the Cloudtanic or financing its conversion and that started him having second thoughts. Eddie could see that he was looking perplexed and enquired why.

"I really hadn't considered buying the machine. I've only just bought a new model; I simply don't have the cash."

"You leave that with me. I'll sort that out."

"But that still leaves the cost of conversion, Eddie."

"Well let's take the idea to Black, Black & Blackemore's and get them to do some design work and get them to quote what a conversion would cost."

Matters rested for now whilst the various parties went about their business and the government cringed as the media had a ball with the mess it had ended up with. In due course, Eddie and Cirrus got together again to discuss where things were at. They pored over the plans that Black, Black & Blackemore's had drawn up for them. They looked pretty impressive.

Essentially, the upper deck had been stripped of all its water storage tanks and refrigerators and a superb apartment, minus any windows, had been installed. The outside world could be viewed on a TV screen and PPI. It was all just like Cirrus had thought it should be, except that a bar and small gymnasium had been included.

"That all looks fabulous but how much will it cost?"

"That's all taken care of; you don't have a thing to worry about."

"How have you managed that, Eddie?" enquired an unbelieving Cirrus.

"A firm from Portrush in Northern Ireland has agreed to purchase the machine from the government and to fund the conversion work."

Cirrus had an idea who that could be.

"It wasn't the Riley Academy by any chance?"

"So it is Cirrus, but the Academy has made two conditions."

"Go on!"

"First, you must engage a good chef and second, you have to take on one member of their staff as a member of your crew."

"The first condition isn't a problem but who is the person we have to take on as crew?"

"I didn't catch her full name but I believe she is called Venus."

Cirrus nearly fell off his seat at the mention of her name but regained his composure just as Eddie continued.

"You better think about planning an itinerary and how you are going to advertise your cloud cruise holidays."

Once Eddie had left, Cirrus couldn't wait to tell Puffy the latest news and when he did his eyes lit up like two light bulbs. Venus was enough to set any man on fire. The problem was, however, where would she be accommodated on board and what would she do as a crew member? Poor Josh got the push.

The Relaunch

Black, Black & Blackemore's did a splendid job converting the Cloudtanic into a cruise cloud and it was decided that it should be re-launched at Wythenshawe Weather Centre. It was to be a similar ceremony to the previous one except that the invited dignitaries would not be government ministers.

Wythenshawe's huge hangar was suitably cleaned for the occasion and everything was set out as before. Wingates Band provided the musical entertainment and a large number of cloud owners were present to witness the re-launch. Cloud crews were just as superstitious as ship's crews and a launch was regarded as extremely important.

It looked as if a new name had been painted on the nose of the craft but it had been covered over. The 'Guild of Cloud Owners' President, George Fowlup CDM, was on the launch platform along with the Centre's Superintendent, Mr Ivor N. Spite CDM, and in between the pair of them was Joe Riley from the Riley Academy in Portrush and a gorgeous young lady called Venus.

The music stopped and the Guild's President stepped up to the microphone to address those gathered.

"Ladies, Gentlemen and fellow Cloud Owners, it is my pleasure today to invite Mr Joe Riley from the Riley Academy to step forward and launch this new cloud machine which will see in a new era of work for all of us. In the future, we may be able to add weather cruises to our weather-making CV."

When it became obvious that Mr Fowlup was not going to say anything else, applause broke out and then he spoke again.

"May I ask Mr Riley to name our new craft?"

Joe stumbled forward before grabbing a magnum of champagne that had been strategically placed on the platform whilst Mr Spite grabbed the end of a cord attached to the canvas cover.

"Oi name this cloud machine Gondalus *an good luck oi say to all who cruise holiday in her."*

With the magnum of champagne in his right hand, Joe wobbled nearer the craft and swung it with some force so that it impacted hard on the nose creating a large dent. Mr Spite pulled the cord to reveal the name *Gondalus,* at which point everyone stood and clapped. Wingates Band struck up with a suitable number as the newly named cruise machine was towed out of the hangar and into the sunshine.

The audience made a rapid exit for the Silver Lining Club where the topic of conversation surrounded Wingates Band's rendition of 'What shall we do with the drunken sailor,' which had fortuitously turned out to be most opportune.

Whilst most of those present had headed for the Silver Lining Club, Cirrus, Puffy, Abigail and Venus escorted the *Gondalus* out into the sunshine and admired its new dent.

"What happens next, skipper?" asked Puffy.

"We will have to learn how to operate it and work as a four man team."

"Don't forget, Cirrus, that we are not all men," said Abigail.

Looking at Venus, Puffy couldn't help feeling that there was no chance of that.

"Point taken, Abigail! Tomorrow we will be flown to Bishops Court to complete a conversion course and then we can get cruising," remarked Cirrus.

"Has the business been advertised yet?" asked Puffy.

Not yet and I haven't organised a cordon bleu chef either, but I will.

The four of them left the dented *Gondalus* where it was and headed to join everyone else in the Silver Lining Club. Cirrus ambled alongside Puffy and whispered to him,

"I don't think it will be a good idea for your wife and Venus to both be onboard at the same time. It's just asking for trouble."

"Don't you worry about that, skipper! The wife's left me again!"

A couple of days later, the first crew of the *Gondalus* stepped aboard the craft which was about to be flown to Bishops Court by Black, Black & Blackemore's test pilot, Johnny Black, and test engineer, Ronnie Blackemore. The flight was uneventful in the darkness of night and appeared to be no different from being in the Nimbus, thought Cirrus. On landing, the craft was taxied into a hangar, out of the way of prying eyes. Conversion training would begin the following evening.

The following day presented an opportunity to explore the layout of the new machine. The lower deck was identical to existing cloud machines with the exception that in the cockpit area the drop-down bunks had gone and a spiral staircase had been fitted to give access to the upper deck. Having ascended the staircase, a corridor led to the passenger suite and as it did so, it passed the crew compartment which included sleeping accommodation for five, a shower and toilet and a galley-come-dining area. It was a leap forward from the facilities aboard the Nimbus.

Proceeding down the corridor, the passenger suite was reached and beyond the entry door the contrast in fittings was truly remarkable. There was a feeling of opulence about the accommodation. The lounge and dining area looked splendid with its royal décor. Two TV screens were fixed into the side wall, one for viewing the outside world and one for TV programmes and DVDs. A PPI had also been installed to enable cruise passengers to see where they were geographically. Moving on from the lounge, a miniature gym had been installed and next to it was a shower and toilet. Then came the bedroom and it was most tempting to try out the huge comfortable looking bed in a setting splendidly decorated. There was immediate agreement between all four crew members that the manufacturers had done a great job. Now it was time to get on with the training.

For the two pilots, Cirrus and Abigail, the conversion course had nothing new to offer. The *Gondalus* had a flight deck with exactly the same controls and dials as their own machines and hence it was not a challenge. The machine seemed to handle the same as well and it was no time at all before the examiners at Bishops Court were satisfied that they were both competent and signed off their licences appropriately.

With all the extra water storage tanks and refrigerators on the top deck removed, the flight engineer's station was changed little. A few fuel tank gauges and selectors had been added for the extra external storage tanks but that was no burden for Puffy. Venus, on the other hand, was starting from scratch and it was her ability to master the task at hand that determined the duration of the course, but no-one pressured her, especially Puffy who was giving her as much attention as the Centre's Instructors. His attention was not always cruise cloud machine orientated. With a background of hotel work, Venus found her new source of work challenging to say the least but it was totally absorbing and a great change. The extra attention she was getting from Puffy was also flattering, she thought, and she was fitting in well with the others.

In the beginning, the *Gondalus* was confined to flying in the dark but that soon changed when Venus felt confident enough to initiate atomising. The cloud she created immersed the machine in vapour, making it invisible from the ground, and daytime flying became a reality. As soon as she was able to make rain, the cloud could be dispensed with, but only during darkness and then they could land. Landing in daylight with a cloud around the machine was generally frowned upon. Those living in the vicinity of the Training Centre disliked having a mist around for hours on end and it also made movement around the old airfield most difficult.

Whilst both the pilots and flight engineers were busy undergoing their conversion course, an effort was being made to find and recruit a cordon bleu chef. It had to be done fast since who ever got the job would need to be signed off as proficient on board the *Gondalus* and that could only be done at Bishops Court. This was going to be a history-making appointment since no chef had ever previously been part of a crew.

Several candidates came to Bishops Court for an interview but in the end French –man Pierre Le Blanc was offered the position and he accepted. The choice had been heavily influenced by the quality of his French fries and his general good looks. The latter had much influenced Abigail and Venus who already had her arms around him in her dreams and Puffy got a sense of that. Whether the culinary skills of Pierre would delight any fee-paying cruise cloud passenger remained to be seen but for the moment he was part of the crew and experienced cooking on board a cloud for the first time in his French life.

There was no point in having a cruise cloud and a trained crew without having cruise cloud passengers and only a marketing campaign could achieve that. Joe Riley and Cirrus spent many hours getting their heads around this thorny problem. It probably would have been better if they had employed a professional firm of experts to do this but Joe wanted to keep it in cloud, so to speak. They eventually came up with a plan that covered what they would offer and how much they would charge and then started to turn their thoughts to getting the word out.

Advertising on television and radio featured strongly in the marketing plan alongside the creation of a poster to display in travel agents and anywhere that they could be put on a public poster-board. More advertising would be done in newspapers and magazines. Even an online advert would feature in the all-embracing attempt to attract fee paying cruise cloud passengers.

Joe was anxious to ensure that the project was financially self-supporting and not a drain on his monetary resources. The creation of a separate business was most important to him and, given that he had purchased the *Gondalus* and funded the conversion work, he felt that for tax purposes it would be better in the name of Cirrus. Cirrus was a little nervous to go down this road but when he had been reassured that it would not risk his own meagre finances he acceded to Joe's wishes. After further protracted negotiations, the new company was called ***Cirrus Airwaves.***

Within due course the marketing campaign got underway and the new company appeared on TV and was heard on the radio. Posters appeared all over the place and people could see it advertised in the newspapers and in magazines. It was all done to create a big impact and it certainly became a big talking point amongst the general public.

Down in the Slaidburn watering hole, the 'Hark to Bounty', to give it its proper title, the locals couldn't resist having a go at Cirrus whenever he joined them for a pint.

"What's all this honeymoon business you are going into Cirrus. It's a bit different isn't it, from your normal work?"

"It's a holiday in a cruise cloud," replied Cirrus.

"It's a bit expensive isn't it?"

"What do you expect? It's an upmarket cruise for two."

"Upmarket cruise for two, I'll bet it's for them toffs who want a couple of weeks away with their secretary in a place where they can't be found."

That hadn't really occurred to Cirrus. When he thought about it he didn't really want to be associated with providing a service for such an activity but Puffy thought it was probably the most likely source of passengers they would get. Abigail tended to side with Cirrus whilst Venus sided with Pierre. His left side to be precise, and his left shoulder as well.

"Ere, Puffy. Why don't you get Carol on it? Maybe you can get back with her if you treat her to a holiday."

Puffy didn't reply. His left side was suffering from the absence of Venus and the only thing he could think of was getting Pierre to burn his chips. This was not how he had hoped things would turn out.

"Has Cirrus Airwaves got a booking yet?" asked one of the more nosey locals, but Cirrus didn't have an answer for that and he wished he had.

Cirrus Airwaves

Announces its new season of cloud cruises aboard the *Gondalus*.

Ever fancied cruising in the heavens at a leisurely pace in
a luxurious cabin with your own cordon bleu chef?

Why not consider ascending into the sky to join nature's cavalcade of
white wonders casually blowing around the four corners of the globe?

For a couple who like to try something different,
this could be your dream cloud come true!

For a couple who prefer to holiday in private,
the sky is a place no-one will invade.

**Wanting to honeymoon – you can't get
any higher than a cloud cruise!**

Cloud cruises can be tailored to suit your individual requirements.

For those wishing for a pre-planned itinerary, why not consider cruising
around the UK coastline and viewing it from a bird's eye position before
dropping in each night to a fresh location?

Interested?

Call 0569 – 2876 – 1212 for further details and terms

The First Cloud Cruise

Charles and Sophie McDougal had always had a dream about returning to their family roots. Life in New York must be so different from that in Scotland, the place their ancestors had left during the Highland clearances. That was a long time ago and long enough to generate a strong urge to return. Life in the USA had been good and the McDougals were pretty well-off for money. They could afford to be extravagant when it came to choosing someplace to go for a honeymoon but they also wanted to do something no-one else had done before, something that they could spend a lifetime bragging about.

One Sunday morning in his New York apartment, Charles was doing his regular Sunday morning thing by reading the New York Herald but it was not until he got to the centre pages that he spotted the advert by Cirrus Airwaves. He couldn't believe what he read and read it several more times before reaching the conclusion that this was just what he had been looking for. At first he toyed with the idea of ringing Sophie but then he thought twice about it. This could be a wonderful surprise for her.

"Hello, this is Cirrus Airwaves, how can I help you?"

"My name is Charles McDougal and I'm calling from New York."

"How can I help you, Mr McDougal?"

"I've just seen your ad in the New York Herald and it sure looks interesting."

"I'm very pleased that you think so sir," replied Cirrus who was already anticipating a customer.

"I'm gonna get married in a couple of weeks an I'm lookin fer somethin different fer a honeymoon.

"Cirrus Airwaves can offer lots of different things. Do you have anything in mind?"

"Well me an my girl, we both have ancestors that come from Scotland an I want to visit the place on our honeymoon."

Phone calls were switched to e-mails and many passed back and forth before a tailor- made itinerary was established and a fee negotiated. The fee was quite substantial since it was most involved but it was agreed. Nothing was too much for Charles' fiancée, Sophie.

A good many arrangements had to be made with boat owners in a number of Scottish locations and a guide was hired at one of them. For Cirrus and Abigail there was a tremendous amount of detail to be planned not just from a navigation point of view but more to do with timings. Venus and Puffy had to be fully briefed and Pierre had the job of stocking up with food of good quality. There would be an opportunity for fresh food to be brought aboard at several locations but it would involve extra arrangements being made with boat owners.

Charles and Sophie flew to Manchester immediately after their marriage and were met on arrival by Puffy who then drove them the short distance to Wythenshawe Weather Centre. First impressions of the place were not good. Dominated by a huge hangar and an unimpressive looking admin building, the establishment was not inspiring and Charles had a twinge of anxiety. Puffy drove them straight into the hangar where the *Gondalus* and the rest of its crew were waiting.

"Honey, look at that thing!"

"What is it, Charles?"

"It's the craft that's gonna take us around Scotland, honey."

Sophie shrieked in excitement and the sound was very piercing to Puffy's ears.

The car was brought to halt close to the entrance to the *Gondalus* and Abigail stepped forward to open the car door. Charles stepped out, followed by Sophie, and Cirrus introduced himself before introducing Venus and Pierre, and Abigail introduced herself after Cirrus had forgotten her.

The newly-weds were taken aboard the craft and led to the cockpit area before ascending the steps to the top deck which would be their home for the next couple of weeks. On entering their cabin they were taken aback by the sheer magnificence of everything. A bottle of champagne was opened by Pierre and they were left to enjoy it and get accustomed to their new surroundings.

"Wad do you think of it, Honey?"

"Its fabulous, Charles, but what are we going to do in it?"

Charles thought a demonstration was better than words and he led her to the bedroom.

Now that everyone was aboard there was little to do but wait until it was dark and then they could get airborne. Pierre busied himself preparing a cordon bleu meal for his American passengers whilst Puffy did the microwaving stuff for the rest of the crew.

By 9-00pm it was dark enough to get airborne and the honeymooners were asked if they would like to come down onto the flight deck and watch the take-off, but they couldn't be raised on the inter-com. The four fan duct motors were started and the *Gondalus* taxied forward before turning towards the hangar doors. The lights in the hangar started to dim and finally went out as the big doors opened. Out on the concrete apron, Cirrus checked that everything was working ok and Puffy did the same at his flight engineer's station. A call was then made to Wythenshawe Control and permission was granted for take-off.

The *Gondalus* ascended rapidly into the night sky and didn't stop until it had reached 5,000 feet, at which height Cirrus activated his ID beacon before heading in the darkness for the Irish Sea. Sophie had never experienced such a feeling in bed as that engendered by the ascending *Gondulas* and Charles shared praise for a performance that was not truly of his own making but he didn't let on.

Once over the Irish Sea, Cirrus brought the *Gondalus* to a hover in order that Puffy could initiate the atomising process. Within thirty minutes the *Gondalus* created a Westmorland White cloud around itself that would give it anonymity in the sky. This was a cloud that, unlike its neighbours would have an endless existence as long as it was needed for cover. Although its life would end as rain, it would have served a noble purpose.

Cirrus headed the cruise cloud across the Irish Sea to Douglas in the Isle-of-Man where, on arrival, he would hover over the bay until his passengers went ashore. The flight into a westerly headwind was pretty routine except that nature's convoy was going the other way. That didn't matter too much since most of it was below them masking their track to a large extent from humanity and there wasn't much of that on the Irish Sea.

Eventually Charles and Sophie came down onto the flight deck to take a look at what was happening. They could see Douglas on the TV screen, just as they had done in their cabin. Cirrus explained to them how the PPI was indicating their position over Douglas Bay and then offered them the opportunity of going ashore for a few hours. Sophie jumped at the idea and Cirrus started the slow descent whilst Puffy contacted the local boatman whom they had an agreement with.

Difficulties in Douglas

Holidaymakers in Douglas were enjoying a day in the sun before the *Gondalus* arrived and altered everything. Whilst the craft hovered a foot or so above sea level its cloud extended out a considerable distance embracing, as it did so, the beach, promenade and a good half of the town. There is a massive difference between playing on a sun baked beach and getting damp in a thick mist and it was not appreciated by Douglas' visitors.

Boats coming and going from the harbour did more anchor-dropping than going and it wasn't long before all sea travel was temporarily brought to a halt except in the case of the boat hired by Cirrus Airwaves.

Whilst Charles and Sophie waited patiently for their ferry boat to take them to visit Douglas, the boatman was having a difficult time of it finding them in this damned mist. After almost an hour of going round in circles, he was on the verge of giving up when his boat bumped into the *Gondalus*. Eventually the entry door was located and it opened followed by the extension of the access ladder and the newly-weds were able to go aboard for the short journey to the mainland. Short it may have been but that damned mist didn't help and the short journey became a long one.

When it did arrive in Douglas it was not where it should have been but for the moment the beach was as good as anywhere.

Going ashore with soaking wet shoes and socks is not a good start to looking around and neither is looking around a mist covered town. Things were not getting off to a good start. During the several hours that the two Americans spent looking around, the *Gondalus* just stayed where it was and waited and held up all sea travel to and from Douglas as it did so. The Liverpool to Douglas ferry had to hold offshore and wait for what it thought was a mist to lift, and its passengers were not very happy with the delay.

After several mist-filled hours in Douglas, Charles and Sophie had seen enough of what little they could see and headed for the beach to find the boat that would take them back to the *Gondalus*. That was easier said than done and it took another full hour to find it, by which time their clothing was impregnated with cold moisture causing them to shiver almost uncontrollably. All this discomfort was not helped when the boat got underway. Getting underway was simple but underway to where? The boatman had no idea where in the mist the *Gondalus* loitered and a further hour was spent going around in it and it was beginning to go dark. By a great stroke of luck they bumped into the mist covered craft and set about locating the access door.

Charles and Sophie did not present a pretty sight as they came aboard the *Gondalus*. Wet, bedraggled and shivering, they were escorted to their luxury cabin and Pierre was given instructions to look after them in the best way he knew how and, being a cordon bleu chef, he cooked them a magnificent meal.

On the flightdeck, Cirrus and Abigail looked at each other worriedly.

"That doesn't look as if it has been too successful," remarked Cirrus.

"You are absolutely right, Cirrus. We are going to have to change a few things as we go along," replied Abigail.

The *Gondalus* lifted off from Douglas Bay taking its cloud with it which allowed the Liverpool to Douglas ferry to enter harbour, much to the relief of its passengers. Douglas soon returned to normal as the mist lifted but it had been an inconvenience and, generally, not appreciated.

The next port of call was Bangor in Northern Ireland where the whole disastrous performance was repeated and then it was on to Campbeltown on the Mull-of-Galloway. Charles and Sophie refused to go ashore at Campbeltown fearing another repeat performance. It had been accepted as funny at first but twice was a bit much and three times was just diabolical. Clearly things had to change and they would, but not before the next destination.

Oban awaited and Oban got it, the *Gondalus* that is. It descended to a position just offshore, shrouding the place in mist just as before. This time, however, the boatman setting out had a portable radio and a GPS set which had the co-ordinates of the position of the *Gondalus* punched in when the boatman had received them over the radio. It was just a question then of using his compass to reach the craft and the short journey was performed in a short time. The return to the *Gondalus* was equally efficient and both Cirrus and Abigail could heave a sigh of relief on that score.

Oban experienced the same inconvenience as Douglas had. All sea travel came to a halt for the several hours that the mist sat where it was and that was not going down well with ferries that come and go to Oban. This Scottish town already got its fair share of mist and another one, even if it brought two American tourists with it, was not wanted. Damp tourists don't tend to stay and when they don't stay they don't spend, and that was not popular with the town council.

Complaints were beginning to mount up as various mist-hit locations conferred. Cirrus Airwaves could take its mist somewhere else; it was not welcome in Scotland. Cirrus had to stress to the crew that this must be kept from their fare-paying passengers at all costs.

The *Gondalus* moved on to Portree on the Isle-of-Skye and then to Stornoway on the Isle-of-Lewis. The same issues occurred again and their mist was becoming evermore a huge headache. No-one wanted a mist that put a damper on their tourists and played havoc with shipping and it was particularly objectionable if you wore a kilt. Mists get to places most unwanted and up a kilt is one of them. Another rethink was required to get this cloud cruise to a more practical level of acceptability.

Charles and Sophie enjoyed the privacy of their luxurious cabin and the excellent cordon bleu cooking. They enjoyed going onto the flight-deck to watch their arrival at each destination on the TV screen. They didn't mind a short trip through the mist to a new venue but they didn't care much for walking round a place in a mist. The first venue they had visited, Douglas, the mist had been a novelty but when it occurred at every venue, well that was simply absurd. The only consolation had been snuggling up in bed afterwards to get warm, or so they said. The point about all this was that the current plan was not working.

Arrival at Wick brought a new approach to things. Once the *Gondalus* had descended to sea level and discharged its passengers into a waiting boat, it ascended again and hovered several thousand feet above. Wick was saved a mist although it got a shade as a replacement but that was a lot better and that was a great relief to everyone, and Charles and Sophie enjoyed their visit ashore much more being mist free.

Banff, Arbroath and North Berwick followed and things seemed to be working well. There were murmurings, however, questioning the acceptability of Scotland having to endure a host of shades in order that a couple of American tourists can sight-see, but they were only murmurs. A lot of American tourists visit Scotland.

The last destination was to be Berwick-on-Tweed and a slightly different set of arrangements had been put in place. Instead of the *Gondalus* descending to sea level offshore and rendezvousing with a boat, it would descend to ground level on the edge of the town. There, a guide would meet Charles and Sophie as they disembarked and escort them through the mist and into town.

Right on the agreed time, the *Gondalus* descended with its cloud around it and landed exactly on target. Charles and Sophie were escorted to the exit door which was opened to reveal the outside mist. The access ladders were lowered and the newly-weds stepped down to ground level to meet their guide. They were bid farewell by Venus who reminded them of the time they would be picked up. With that the exit door was closed and Charles and Sophie were left to their own mist.

The guide never showed up or never found Charles and Sophie and after waiting for a considerable time they decided to try and find their own way out of the mist they were in. That took an inordinate amount of time and they were extremely frustrated to watch the mist lift just as they had reached its edge. The guide was no-where to be seen.

"Sophie, I ain't gonna try and find that dam Gondalus through that dam mist when we are due back."

"What are we gonna do, Charles?"

"Sophie, we are gonna get a train back to Manchester. Ah have just about had enough of this dam Scotch mist business. Ma ancestors can keep it!"

"Oh Charles, I do love ya when you are so strong and decisive."

When the *Gondalus* returned several hours later, Charles and Sophie didn't appear and, whilst waiting, Puffy received a phone call from Joe Riley.

"Skipper, Joe Riley has just been on the phone and says we are to make our way back to Wythenshawe."

"What about Charles and Sophie?"

"He says they won't come back aboard. They are taking a train back to Manchester."

That didn't sound good, thought Cirrus, and he ascended back into the sky, taking his mist with him, and then proceeded to Wythenshawe via Liverpool Bay where they rained.

The inquest with Joe did not go well but they didn't fall out. It transpired that Charles had been texting back home on a daily basis and the stories he told of his honeymoon cloud cruise were making interesting reading. Any further business headed in the direction of Cirrus Airwaves was now pointing in a different direction and a passenger famine was fast approaching. It was agreed that many of the problems encountered should have been foreseen. It had been a disaster ironing things out as they occurred and now the penalty had to be paid. Cirrus Airwaves was wound up and the *Gondalus* confined to the scrap heap. Pierre became unemployed but he got a Venus as a bonus. As for Cirrus, Abigail and Puffy, well it was back to the business of good old fashioned weather-making and delivery for them and not so much of the 'other things'.

TUPPENCE A SHOWER

Alf Wilmot and his family had lived in Great Yarmouth all their lives and his family roots could be traced back in the town for over one hundred years. Successive generations of the Wilmot family had been involved in the entertainments business but Alf could only manage an arcade of slot machines which he was still immensely proud of. 'Wilmot's Winning Slot Machines' provided a source of fun on Great Yarmouth's promenade and was something of a traditional attraction for the many visitors that travelled here. Old and young alike loved the opportunity to have a little gamble, safe in the knowledge that it was extremely unlikely that they would lose vast amounts of money.

Wilmot's arcade was not the only one on Great Yarmouth's promenade but few others could match its longevity. One that could belonged to Ben Capstick, who, like the Wilmots, had a family connection with the town going back to the nineteenth century. Ben came from a family with a long military connection. His late father had left the Army in 1946 after twenty-five years service. He had no trade to speak of other than soldiering and had taken a gamble in the year of his discharge by buying an arcade. He had taken a chance on the revival of holidaymaking and his chance had been well rewarded over the years. When Ben's father passed away, he inherited the arcade which provided him with a comfortable living. As in the Wilmot place, slot machines abounded and literally thousands of holidaymakers tried their luck on them each year.

Alfie Wilmot and Ben Capstick competed with each other, along with one or two other arcade owners, but they did so without any malice. Alf and Ben got on well with each other and their families had been friends for many years. It was not unusual for the two families to help each other out whenever the need arose. A friendly rivalry had built up over the years and it was customary to see who could attract the most visitors over a typical holiday season. Whilst one or other family would celebrate success toward the end of a year, it was always done in the company of both, and each shared in the outcome with a pledge by the loser to be the winner next time.

The two family arcades had tried many different tactics over the years to guarantee success in attracting the most punters. In the early days these had not been particularly innovative. Both had a kept an eye out for new machines under development and whenever something new had come onto the market it was sure to be seen in one or other of the two arcades. At least they kept up to date but there was a limit to the pulling power of new slot machines. Things did get a bit more serious when they started to run out of ideas and initially they resorted to increasing the percentage of payouts from their 'one-armed bandits' as the machines have become known. This was, however, a tricky road to go down since it could impact unfavourably on their incomes and when it did so, a truce was called before it became too late.

To get one over on the other was going to take something a bit more creative. Each arcade was pretty substantial in size and there was scope, size-wise, for the places to accommodate alternative things. It was the Wilmots who pioneered the idea of establishing a cafeteria in their arcade and it soon flourished. Great Yarmouth's holidaymakers put a seal of success on it and it rapidly became clear that the Capsticks were going to lose out unless they followed suit which they did and the status quo was re-established. Not to be outdone, the Capsticks had the idea of installing a bar but this was not free from complications. Getting a licence to sell alcohol proved exceedingly difficult. The local authority was not overly keen on the idea of alcohol being available in places where a high number of young people go but they relented when a number of safeguards had been put in place. The selling of alcohol was not as successful in attracting extra punters as the cafeteria and whilst the Wilmots felt obliged to follow suit, neither business felt any great benefit. In fact, they both experienced unwanted altercations from a combination of drunks and youngsters who had been refused purchase. Both establishments were in danger of getting a bad reputation and the bars were disposed of before the police had them closed.

It had often been noticed that many folks calling in the arcades would have spent more if they had brought more money with them and although that may sound obvious, it was often down to the fact that they had not been to the bank before calling in. What better than to get a bank cash machine in the place, thought Alf. Negotiations went on between Alf, the banks and the local authority for a considerable period of time but in the end a machine was installed and takings rapidly increased. Ben was forced to follow that one up but he went one better by arranging that cash machine payouts could be in pennies and it wasn't long before punters could be observed walking around with enormously bulging pockets. Strangely, after an unprecedented spate of muggings, they all came to a stop and the police concluded it was because the takings never amounted to much, just an enormous number of pennies.

Somehow it seemed as if it was Alf's turn to come up with something new but he was blowed if he could think of anything. He had been to his local pub one evening for a pint, telling his wife that he was looking for some inspiration. He said that every Friday night and he never came back with any. The pub was bristling with folk that Alf knew and although he exchanged pleasantries with them all, he seriously wanted a quiet corner and a pint whilst he gave serious consideration to any possible new innovations. After three pints, he gave up on inspiration and settled for drinking which was much easier but more expensive.

As Alf stepped out through the pub door it started to rain. It only lasted for about thirty seconds but it was enough for him to remember something he had seen in the paper a week or so previously. As he stepped through his front door he called for his wife and asked her where the paper might be. There was a good chance it had been thrown out, but his wife, Christine, remembered it distinctly. Alf had brought a particularly funny advert to her attention. She hadn't thrown it out and Alf was delighted. He rummaged through the pages until he came upon what he was looking for and here it was.

Hire a Downpour

He had just found the inspiration he was looking for! It had been at home all the time but he had still enjoyed his pint in the pub.

Cirrus is in a Huff

It's not going to be another of those mornings, thought Puffy as he stood outside the lounge door with a cup of coffee in hand. He could hear his skipper grunting and groaning and recognised these as signs that he had, once more, found something to his distaste in the morning paper.

"I wish he wouldn't get too engrossed in the Daily Gloom," Puffy said to himself. *"They don't always tell the true story,"* he continued as he plucked up the courage to face the inevitable barrage of his plagued skipper.

"Ah there you are, Puffy, and coffee in hand. Excellent, just what I needed."

That was not the response that Puffy had expected but it was most welcome.

"Not found anything interesting in the paper this morning, Captain?"

That was a huge mistake for it opened the flood doors and the opinions came pouring out.

"You know, Puffy, I really can't see where this country is going when it comes to the law."

Puffy didn't really want to respond but felt that he had an obligation to do so, and so he did.

"What makes you say that, Captain?"

"Well just listen to this: a chap in Lincolnshire is in bed with his wife and his sleep is disturbed in the early hours by sounds downstairs, and so he gets up, scared stiff, and makes his way quietly, to investigate what's going on. He arms himself with a pan from the kitchen before entering the room that the noise is coming from."

The tension was building up as Puffy eagerly awaited the next bit.

"The chap confronts a burglar in the dark and, in the heat of the moment, hits him with the pan and lays him clean out."

"I'll bet that was a relief," said Puffy.

"It was, until the police arrived."

"Why, what happened then?"

"They arrested the house owner for using excessive force."

"That can't be right!" said Puffy.

"It can't be right in the eyes of you or me or Joe Public, but in the eyes of the law, well that's altogether a different thing.

After a slight pause, Puffy was about to make his escape but as he made his first move towards the door his Captain spouted forth on another matter.

"And just look at this bloke here from overseas. He arrives in the country, supposedly to study, and commits one crime after another. When he gets caught he can't be deported because it will infringe his human rights."

Puffy was wise enough this time not to appear overly interested for it would only encourage Cirrus even more. It made no difference, however.

"And another thing: who pays for this bloke to be cared for, as he languishes in prison? It costs the country an absolute fortune and there is nothing we can do about it until we get out of the European Union."

This was a danger point! When Cirrus got on about the EU the debate could escalate, especially since the business associated with the *Cloudtanic*.

Cirrus was about to kick-off again when the post could be heard dropping through the letter-box. Puffy was saved by the postie and beat a hasty retreat.

The arrival of the latest edition of the Monthly Downpour proved to be Puffy's salvation as his skipper began to read it. The monthly journal, produced by the 'Guild-of-Cloud Owners', was avidly read by all those involved in the weather-making business. It provided a link between all those cloud machine owners going about their worldly work, who rarely had an opportunity to come together at their headquarters in Wythenshawe. The journal kept everybody up to date with personal matters such as weddings, births and deaths, whilst on the work side of things one could read about cloud machine developments, training courses and awards, not to mention jobs on offer. On the social side, functions in the Silver Lining Club were often to be found amongst the many pages.

Cirrus gave the journal a quick scan before settling on the jobs on offer section. His attention was caught by the requirement for 'thirty second showers on demand'. He was intrigued by this and read further. There wasn't a lot of detail except to say that it would embrace a summer season at Great Yarmouth in Norfolk. If any further details were required then enquiries were to be made to the Superintendent's secretary at Wythenshawe Weather Centre.

Cirrus was interested in the idea of providing thirty second showers on demand and decided he would give the Superintendent's secretary a ring, but before that he would return to his copy of the Daily Gloom and consult the stars to see what they predicted for him. This was a routine that he followed on a daily basis when he was not delivering weather and it was a great source of amusement to Puffy.

In due course a call was made to Wythenshawe and Goldilocks answered.

"And how is Mr Spite's secretary today?" enquired Cirrus.

"I'm very well thank you, Captain Cumulus. What can I do for you?"

"I noticed that job in Great Yarmouth in the Monthly Downpour and wondered what else you can tell me about it?"

"I can't tell you an awful lot more. It will last for a full holiday season and the fee is very good. The chap who requires the showers is called Alf Wilmot."

"Can I get in touch with him?"

"I can give you his telephone number if that will help."

Cirrus rang Alf Wilmot who went on to describe his shower requirements and, from Cirrus' point of view, it would be a simple job to perform, the only draw-back being the time the *Nimbus* would have to be on station. Ten solid weeks was a long time to be away and to live in the confined space of the *Nimbus,* let alone the fact that he wouldn't be able to see Abigail in all that time. There would be one day a week off duty, Mondays to be precise, and that would be an opportunity to restock with food and fuel for the fan duct motors but not much else. Nevertheless, the job was easy and paid well and that settled it.

It was assumed that Puffy would have no commitments that would get in the way and when that proved to be the case, the agreement was made and the *Nimbus* was destined for a season at Great Yarmouth.

A Trial Shower

The crew of the Nimbus arrived at Wythenshawe Weather Centre and set about checking their cloud machine over in the vast hangar. When satisfied that everything was functioning, it was time to stock up with supplies and then to top up the fuel tanks. It was then time to wait until it got dark and the time seemed to pass very slowly. There was no-one around apart from themselves in the hangar. It looked as if all the other cloud machine owners were away on weather business, the majority, no doubt, on one of Eddie Stormbart's foreign aid convoys.

When it did eventually start going dark, Cirrus and his Flight Engineer, Puffy, boarded the Nimbus and took up their positions in the cockpit. The four fan duct motors were started and, when it was time to depart, the Nimbus moved forward before turning to face the hangar door. As it did so, the doors started to open and the internal hangar lights started to dim.

As the nose of the Nimbus reached the doors, the internal hangar lights had completely extinguished and the machine taxied out into the darkness for a short distance and then stopped. Cirrus checked his instruments to ensure everything was working fine before getting Puffy to contact Wythenshawe control for clearance to take off. They had to wait a few minutes as a large passenger aircraft flew over the Weather Centre on its final approach to land at nearby Manchester Airport. With that out of the way they were cleared for take off.

The four fan duct motors were wound up and Cirrus pulled back on his control column to alter the angle of the motors to provide lift and the Nimbus literally leapt into the night sky. The vertical climb to five thousand feet was achieved in no time at all which was just as well since another passenger aircraft was about to pass over the Weather Centre on its landing approach into the airport.

Leveling out at five thousand feet, Cirrus couldn't help wondering about the wisdom of establishing a weather centre for cloud machines directly under the flight approach path into a busy airport. Wondering over, it was time to switch on the ID beacon and then head off in the direction of Liverpool and the Irish Sea. There was a light westerly wind blowing and nature's puffy jobs were all scudding east but they were scattered, leaving hundreds of gaps through which the twinkling lights of mother earth's inhabitants could be viewed. It was vistas like this that gave Cirrus, and Puffy for that matter, a great deal of delight. This kind of detachment from all below gave them a kind of feeling that they were spiritual observers, but they soon got back to reality as Liverpool appeared ahead. It didn't take much longer before the Nimbus was brought to a hover and Puffy set his controls to atomise four million gallons of the Irish Sea.

A beautiful Westmorland White cloud was created around the Nimbus which, from now on, would be invisible to the world. Apart from creating the cloud some of the atomised sea water was turned back again into water for storing in the craft's water tanks and some of it was frozen to be stored as ice in the craft's refrigerators. It took about an hour for this process to be completed, at which point Cirrus turned his lovely white cloud onto a heading for Cromer on the north coast of Norfolk. They would be on a track that would take them diagonally across the paths of nature's wonders but in the dark that mattered little. The journey to Cromer would take several hours and that gave the crew a chance to relax a little. In the darkness, the view outside was provided by the pop-up TV screen on the flight deck and it seemed strange being on a collision course with another cloud and then flying straight through it without a bump or any other feeling of impact and then to emerge clear of it into a large black space of night sky. This wondrous kind of journey never failed to impart a feeling of incredulity in spite of it being repeated again and again over the years. Nature's beauty was truly astounding, thought Cirrus.

"Why are we going to Cromer and not Great Yarmouth, skipper?" asked Puffy.

"As far as I am aware, Alf Wilmot wants us to do a trial shower at Cromer."

"You mean he wants to make sure it works ok before showering Great Yarmouth?"

"That's the top and shower of it," replied Cirrus.

"What exactly do we have to do?" enquired Puffy.

"We hover over Cromer and when we receive a radio signal we give the place a light shower for exactly thirty seconds and we repeat that every time we receive a signal."

"What's it all in aid of skipper?"

"Puffy, I have absolutely no idea what it's all in aid of. It's just another job as far as we are concerned."

The early morning light coincided with the Nimbus crossing the Lincolnshire coast at a point south of Skegness, and The Wash and the North Sea came into view as it continued on its path to Cromer. It was time for the crew to contact Alf and let him know that they were almost at their destination. Another forty minutes passed before they arrived and the rented Westmorland White was parked five thousand feet above Cromer awaiting further instructions, but Cromer wasn't aware of it.

The early morning sun, rising in the east, fell on the stationary pearly white cloud at such an angle that its shadow landed at a point several miles further down the coast from Cromer, but it got closer as the day moved on. More important than this right now was the lovely smell of bacon coming from the galley on board the Nimbus. Puffy was at work and Cirrus sat waiting expectantly for breakfast and he wasn't disappointed when it came.

One of the great things about delivering weather, thought Puffy, was the fact that his skipper didn't get the chance to top up his depression by reading the Daily Gloom and that was most welcome.

"Great breakfast, Puffy! I really enjoyed the bacon."

"What about the tea?" asked Puffy.

"Well you stirred it in the wrong direction," remarked Cirrus.

Blast! I never seem to remember his instructions, thought Puffy. Stir anticlockwise, twelve times at twenty miles per hour. The skipper really is a fussy tea drinker, he thought.

Alf had driven to Cromer and was now standing on its promenade in front of a shop, armed with his small radio transmitter. The shop could represent his arcade in Great Yarmouth, he thought, and his current position replicated that which would be used outside his place. He looked up and he could clearly see his shower source hanging about high above Cromer. His first thought on seeing it was that it was too high up and he called the Nimbus up on his mobile phone.

"Can you get down to one thousand feet?" asked Alf.

The Nimbus slowly descended and as it did so its presence got more noticed and its shadow moved rapidly in the direction of Cromer.

"That's it, ta," said Alf. His message had not gone unheard by some of the locals out shopping and some were already wondering whether there was a link between this chap and the cloud above, but that was too ridiculous to be true and shopping took priority.

"Standby, Puffy! I think the trial is about to start."

Puffy picked up the signal in his headphones and switched on a light drizzle which he carefully timed for thirty seconds before switching it off.

"Well I'll be blessed!" said one of the locals strolling down Cromer's promenade. *"It said nothing about showers on this morning's weather forecast."*

Another passing local replied, *"You can't trust them there forecasters, they frequently get it wrong."* And he carried on his wet way with a wet dog.

Another signal was received and another thirty second shower fell on Cromer and it got quite a few more in the next hour. Alf's loitering outside a shop with a black box in hand did not go unnoticed and several shoppers were gazing at him from inside it. They were beginning to form a connection between Alf's button-pressing on his little black box and the start of a shower, but they couldn't begin believing what appeared to be happening. Meanwhile, Cromer's shoppers who were completely unprepared for showers became adept at dodging them and some shops got some extra business.

As far as Alf was concerned, his idea was working like a dream. This would work well at Great Yarmouth and, judging by the attention he was getting he reckoned it would be a big draw for the holidaymakers. It was the attention he was getting that made him decide to carry on for a bit longer and Cromer got more than its fair share of showers.

The locals may not have been very concerned about the first showers but everyone has a limit and Cromer's was rapidly being reached. A shop full of observers had reached the conclusion that the chap standing outside with a little black box was responsible. Each time he pressed a little red button a short, sharp, shower took place. Some of the observers had taken the risk of exiting their current location at the end of a shower with the purpose of staying dry before dodging indoors again somewhere else. Alf had spotted this tendency and mischievously pressed his red button as they emerged from the shop behind him and he chuckled as they got attacked by his shower.

This simply could not go on and the shop owner called the local police who initially thought that this was a hoax call.

"Now look here dear," said the police constable taking the call. *"Do you really think anybody could switch a shower on and off other than in a bathroom?"*

Norfolk women are made of stern stuff and no police constable was going to insinuate that they were a touch barmy.

It was only a matter of minutes before a police car, siren blaring, came speeding down the promenade before screeching to a halt outside Matthews' Cake shop.

Alf was a little taken aback by the sudden interest being taken in what he was doing, although the interest by the police was not so welcome.

Cirrus could see what was happening on his TV screen and discreetly moved his Westmorland White cloud down the coast in the direction of Great Yarmouth.

"Now look here sir, it has been reported that you are responsible for all these ere showers falling on Cromer and it's causing a lot of bad feeling," said the police constable.

Alf could see that his rented cloud had moved off down the coast and suggested to the police constable that he must be wrong.

"You get him to press that red button on that thing he his holding and you will see if it showers or not," said an irate and wet shopper.

Alf duly pressed the red button for everyone to see and not a single drop of rain fell on Cromer.

"Press it again, go on, press it again."

And Alf did, several times, but nothing fell on Cromer. That was more than can be said for several other places along the coast that the Westmorland White passed over.

"Now look here sir," began the constable. *"It would probably be in your best interest to take your shower and shower somewhere else before I lock you up for investigation."* It was a long shot by the police constable but he had never

booked anyone for showering and he didn't know if it was an offence for that matter.

Alf was satisfied that the trial had gone well and discreetly left Cromer to a shower- free afternoon and hurriedly headed back for Great Yarmouth, but not before calling up the Nimbus and thanking them for a shower well done.

Gamble on a Shower

Posters appeared all around Great Yarmouth announcing Alf Wilmot's latest idea and it attracted considerable interest.

Win a Shower for Tuppence
The only machine of its kind can be found in Wilmot's Arcade
A winning line of three clouds will induce nature to create a shower
All for tuppence in Wilmot's Arcade
Note: Customers are advised to bring an umbrella.

It didn't take long for the local papers to get wind of it and Alf was soon getting enquiries to clarify what his new slot machine could actually do. Most smelled some kind of a scam or that it was a big send up and that he had gone into the bathroom- fitting business. It was however, a local radio interview in which Alf made clear exactly what would happen.

"Mr Wilmot, could you explain to our listeners what it is that is so different about your new slot machine and what it has to do with the weather?" asked the radio station interviewer.

"Well it's like this," began Alf, who then went on, *"Just outside my arcade on the promenade I have a new slot machine that takes two pence pieces. The top prize is achieved when a punter gets a winning line of three clouds."*

"And what happens then Mr Wilmot?"

"Well it starts to rain; you get a shower an all for tuppence!"

"And where does this shower come from Mr Wilmot?"

"Like all of nature's showers it comes from a bloomin cloud!" answered a slightly agitated Alf.

"You mean your slot machine has harnessed one of nature's natural weather forms?"

Alf didn't much care for the way the interview was going. It was making him out as a possible fraud and, whilst in reality he was, he didn't compare himself with a proper cheat and certainly didn't want to be seen as such. But what could he do, he was on air?

"I think you are putting it a bit strong. I'm not in charge of nature but I do know what happens if you get a winning line of three clouds. Why don't you come down to my arcade on the promenade? You know the one 'Wilmot's Winning Slot Machines' arcade and see for yourself?"

With that invitation it was an opportune moment to end the interview and Alf left the radio studio as they played the record 'Over the Rainbow'.

Alf got the publicity he was after and his interview created several articles in the local press extolling the virtues of his new shower-inducing slot machine and all for tuppence. Even the local Tourist Information Office took an interest and leaflets started to appear announcing Great Yarmouth's unique attraction. There is no evidence available as to whether Alf's innovation attracted more holidaymakers to the resort or not but it certainly swelled the number of people coming in to his arcade.

Alf's friend, Ben Capstick, was happy for Alf but not so happy that his arcade was experiencing a drop in punters. Ben was too much of a gentleman to make a fuss about it and decided to simply ride out the showers until they were spent.

The Nimbus spent its nights just offshore and moved to a position over Great Yarmouth each day after receiving a phone call from Alf, and then the day would be spent providing a thirty second shower every time a signal was received from Alf's little black box.

Jamie Ayres, a local schoolboy in his final year, was most grateful to get a summer holiday job but he hadn't quite bargained for what he was going to do. The little black box was a simple enough gadget and all he had to do was stand at the side of a certain slot machine and press the red button every time a line of three clouds occurred. The job was easy but he didn't realise how hemmed in around the machine he would be. Crowds of folk crammed around Alf's latest attraction to get their tuppence worth and Jamie felt their elbows' worth. Apart from the crushing crowd, it was pretty boring after a few hours and even though the pay was good, Jamie didn't think he had the stamina to do it for ten weeks, but time would tell.

One tuppence after another was fed into Alf's shower slot machine but it took some time before the first winning line of three clouds appeared, and as soon as it did the crowd looked expectantly at the cloud that was casting a shadow over Great Yarmouth and it didn't let them down. For a full thirty seconds they experienced the drops of a real wet shower and they cheered and laughed before sticking another succession of tuppences into the machine. A succession of showers followed at varying intervals and each was greeted by loud cheers.

Whilst all this cheering and showering business was going on, a less enthusiastic mass of holidaymakers were less impressed. Great Yarmouth under a cloud was less fun than Great Yarmouth baked in a summer sun and a succession of showers was nothing to write home about. It wasn't long before a fair number of them packed and headed for a less shower-drenched resort. The Tourist Office began to get a little twitchy about extolling the virtues of the resort's tuppeny showers.

Jamie started to get bored with his work and fed up with all the jostling. During what he thought was a long interval between showers he decided to get his own back for being poked in the ribs so often and pressed the red button on his little black box. An unexpected shower took onlookers by surprise but after thirty seconds they turned their attention to feeding the slot machine again. This didn't go unnoticed and Jamie, just for fun, pressed the red button again and a fresh shower was delivered. The crowd was less impressed than before and speculation as to the authenticity of

Alf's wonder machine became rife but they returned to feeding tuppences into it.

Puffy was a little surprised at the frequency at which he had to make a shower for Great Yarmouth but it wasn't for him to question why. It was, however, distinctly odd when a whole succession of signals were received at less than thirty second intervals and the only way he could satisfy demand was to go to continuous rain.

Back on the ground, the crowd lost interest and began to disperse, taking with them the myth that Alf Wilmot had a machine that could deliver a tuppeny shower. Alf came out of his arcade to look up at the cloud he had hired for the job. What in heavens name is going on, he thought, and as he was looking up at it, Jamie Ayres, was disappearing down the promenade in one direction as several members of the Tourist Office were heading in the opposite.

A heated altercation took place and it wasn't long before the police arrived to intervene.

"Now look here, Mr Wilmot, it appears that the only person benefitting from all these showers is you. The rest of Great Yarmouth is fed up with it and a lot of business is going elsewhere."

Alf couldn't understand how so many showers had been won. His machine had been adjusted for a particular ratio of wins and where has Jamie got to, he thought. In spite of his desire to find out what had gone wrong he still had to concede that his idea had drawbacks and his fellow townsfolk were paying the wet price. He concluded that it was his duty to end his money-making idea and dispense with his showers.

And so it came to be in the folklore of Great Yarmouth that there was a time when you could win a tuppeny shower.

WHEN TWO CLOUDS MEET

The crew of the Nimbus decided to take a break in Ballyhalbert after their prolonged time showering at Great Yarmouth. Apart from the rest they would get, they would be free from any nosey enquiries about the weather they had brought to the resort; word gets around fast these days.

The grass on the old airfield just outside the Cumulus retreat looked lovely first thing in the morning with little drops of sparkling dew clinging to each of the green blades. Freshly cut, the grass made the old runway and perimeter track stand out in contrast, although they were beginning to crumble. The derelict control tower stood out in memory of those who had flown from here in the dark days of world war two. Cirrus could never stop himself trying to visualise what it must have been like at the time.

Sharing the company of Puffy, it was inevitable that a conversation would ultimately take place and it was Puffy who started it.

"Captain, do you think you will ever marry that favourite girl of yours?"

Cirrus pondered for a while before he answered.

"I've thought about it more times than I can count."

"Then why don't you take the plunge?"

"That's easier said than done. Abigail is happy with the way things are at present."

"I don't believe that, skipper. Are you sure that there is no other reason?"

Puffy had put Cirrus on the spot but this might not be a bad time to talk straight. The subject would have to be brought up again anyway at some point.

"Abigail has always felt that she did not want to get between us. She knows that we have been close companions for a long time."

Close companions eh, thought Puffy.

"She has no desire to see you having to find separate accommodation and since you and Carol are separated again it puts us back to square one," remarked Cirrus.

A knock on the front door brought the conversation to a premature stop.

"Go and see who it is, Puffy, will you?"

Puffy made his way to the front door and was given a typical greeting as he opened it.

"Top o' the mornin to you! Seamus O'Leary is de name."

"Good morning, Seamus, and what can I do for you?"

"Did you have anyting to do wid dat mist dat brought de Martians to Ballyhalbert?"

Puffy had to think for a while what Seamus was talking about and then it dawned upon him. He must be talking about the time Wally Lenticular dropped in on the old airfield and left his mist-covered *Discovery* parked overnight, but that was a long time ago. He remembered how some local kids had wandered into the mist and got a shock when they bumped into Wally's cloud machine. They had emerged running from it and claiming the Martians had landed. But why was Seamus enquiring about it now? He'd better be careful what he said.

"I do remember the mist now you come to mention it but I didn't have any responsibility for it," remarked Puffy who went on, *"Why do you ask?"*

"Well me son Danny has been a bit deaf ever since and I tought yer might know why."

Puffy had no idea why that might be and suggested it was probably a coincidence.

"It's no bloody coincidence at all. If I get me hands on dose Martians oil give em what for. Anyway, if yer hear anythin will yer let me know? I'm only livin around der corner."

With that, Seamus bade Puffy farewell and made his way home.

Cirrus had been listening to the conversation from the comfort of his lounge chair.

"Did you hear that, skipper?"

"I did indeed and I must say I did think at the time that Wally's flight engineer, Bert Drummond, had been a bit reckless switching on the thunder machine when all those kids had entered his mist."

"Blimey, I had forgotten that. It must have been pretty scary being in the middle of thunder. I dare say that Bert was probably worried they would break things off the Discovery."

"That may be so but the thunder our machines create is fantastically loud."

The conversation reverted to romance and all its complications.

"I don't think you should worry about where I will live if you get married skipper. I might get married myself in the not too distant future."

Cirrus turned to look at Puffy before reminding him of a possible handicap.

"You are already married, Puffy."

After a short bought of coughing, Puffy brought himself around to replying.

"You know that Carol has left me again and I can't keep putting up with all this coming and going business, and anyway, she has another bloke on her arm now. The truth is, I've decided to divorce her."

"On what grounds?" asked Cirrus.

"Desertion, it's as simple as that."

I hope for your sake that it is as simple as that, thought Cirrus.

"Anyway, how will that change anything? You will be officially single and still living with me," remarked a puzzled Cirrus.

"Well I can get hitched again can't I?"

"And I can guess who that will be."

The phone rang and Puffy picked it up. Not much of a conversation seemed to be taking place but whoever was making the call was doing so with a very loud voice, and although Puffy attempted to get a word in here and there he was largely unsuccessful. At the end of the call, Puffy looked ashen-faced and looked into space for some time before he turned to face his Captain.

"That was Carol. She's divorcing me on the grounds of unreasonable behaviour."

"What are you worried about then? That means you will be free to pursue Goldilocks," remarked Cirrus in an attempt to placate him.

"It's not that simple. It's my relationship with Goldilocks that Carol says is unreasonable."

The two men looked at each other in amazement and started to chuckle. It was a chuckle that progressed to a full laugh but neither of them was aware of whether Goldilocks knew anything about it yet and for the moment neither of them thought about it.

A flood brings relief

The doctor in Ballywalter had never come across a case like Danny O'Leary before. According to his father, he had wandered into a mist which had descended on the old aerodrome at nearby Ballyhalbert and had emerged from it partially deaf. On examination, the ex-Army doctor couldn't help thinking that Danny had a form of shell-shock. He had come across many cases of this type during his time in the services. The question, he thought, was how could a mist induce anything like shell-shock?

"Danny, what happened when you entered the cloud?"

"What?"

"Danny, can you tell me what happened when you entered the cloud?"

"What?"

Getting a bit agitated, the doctor tried again but this time he shouted.

"What happened when you went into the mist?"

"Oh. Well oi lost me way."

"Go on. What happened next?"

"Oi bumped into a Martian space ship."

Looking perplexed at this answer the doctor went on, *"How did you know it was a Martian space ship?"*

"Oi taut only de Martians had 'em."

This conversation was going nowhere and the doctor knew it but he tried once more.

"What happened when you found the space ship?"

"Me friend Jimmy tried breaking a piece off as a souvenir."

"And what happened then?"

"Der was a great rumbling noise. It was very loud an me an Jimmy an de rest of der gang, we all legged it out of de ting."

This really was a strange phenomenon. Danny was the fifth young person he had seen this week with the same complaint and the same story. He broke the news to Danny's father that his son had experienced a very loud noise and he told him to stuff a bit of cotton wool in his ear for a couple of weeks and his hearing would probably be ok. It was a bit like shell-shock, he told Seamus.

A few days later, Puffy was busy getting some supplies in Ballyhalbert's only shop when he spotted Seamus having a conversation with another chap and he couldn't resist listening in.

"Oi'l give them Martians a bit of me knuckles if oi get a hold of 'em," said Seamus.

"They'll not get away wid damaging my boy's earing so easily."

"I tink you're right Seamus. My boy got it too. Why don't yer go around to dat fellas who is involved in der wedder business? He must know something."

Puffy beat a hasty retreat on hearing what was transpiring and informed Cirrus as to what he had just overheard. A short time later, a dreaded knock on the door suddenly raised the anxiety level of the crew of the Nimbus as they meekly opened the front door.

"It's Seamus O'Leary again."

That was pretty obvious, they could see him and he was not a welcome sight.

"What can we do for you, Mr O'Leary?"

"My boy an a few udders from de village are all sufferin from shell-shock an dey got it in dat mist dat landed here. Now you two fellas beein in de wedder business might know a ting or two aboot it?"

Cirrus took centre stage and, clearing his throat made it explicitly clear that he and his colleague had nothing to do with the mist that descended on Ballyhalbert and questioned the connection between a mist and shell-shock.

Seamus was in no way satisfied with what he heard.

"I hope you too wedder fellas is not iddin anyting cos if yer ah der will be trouble."

Having made himself clear, Seamus left in a hurry.

"It's getting a bit uncomfortable in Ballyhalbert, skipper," remarked Puffy.

Cirrus was beginning to wish that Wally had never dropped in to visit him but there was nothing he could do about it now.

The phone rang and Puffy answered it. It was Mr Spite's secretary. Before Goldilocks could make clear what she was ringing about, Puffy jumped in.

"I'm terribly sorry that you have been accused of being unreasonable."

"What are you talking about, Puffy?"

A long winded explanation was then forthcoming which left no doubt as to what Carol was accusing the two of them of and which would form the basis of a divorce case. When Goldilocks had calmed down she made it clear that this was not the purpose of the call. A long period of silence ensued and then the phone was put down without another word being uttered by Puffy.

"What was that all about?" asked Cirrus.

"There is some severe flooding in Somerset and Mr Spite wants us to get back to Wythenshawe as soon as we can," replied Puffy.

"Well that's just come in time. It was beginning to get a bit uncomfortable here."

Puffy didn't seem to feel the same sense of relief as his skipper and it didn't go unnoticed.

"Is everything alright, Puffy?"

"Goldilocks is none too pleased about being cited in my divorce."

Cirrus decided that it would be best to leave things as they were and went about getting ready to leave.

The Nimbus had been left stored in a hangar at Newtownards airfield and its crew made the short journey there by car alongside the shore of Strangford Lough. This was a lovely scenic route but the atmosphere today was a little dour. Puffy appeared a bit depressed but that would all change when they got back aboard their cloud machine. They called in a few shops in the town to pick up a few supplies before entering the hangar in which they had parked the Nimbus. Now it was time to check the craft over and then wait for darkness.

The Nimbus emerged from the hangar into the evening's inky blackness and with all four fan duct motors running smoothly it ascended into the night sky without any of the local inhabitants being aware. It continued ascending until Cirrus levelled out at 5,000 feet. The ID beacon was activated and then the craft moved a short distance to hover over Strangford Lough. At this point, Puffy adjusted the relevant controls to atomise a quantity of the Lough and convert it into a Westmorland White cloud that would hide it from humanity; at least it would when it was daylight. All that remained now was for its skipper to punch into the soakometer/navaid the co-ordinates of their present position and that of their destination and off they would go on a south-easterly heading to Wythenshawe Weather Centre.

An unexpected rendezvous

Wally Lenticular and his flight engineer, Bert Drummond, had been engaged to give a lecture on Scotch mist at the University in Dublin. It had been an interesting experience but the audience had felt let down when they couldn't give a demonstration there and then. Clearly, Scotch mist was a serious business in Dublin and not to be taken lightly. In response to a combination of requests and threats, Wally agreed to bring one to the city the following day and that seemed to satisfy everyone.

The crew of the Discovery made their way to the airfield at Baldonnel which was just outside Dublin. The cloud machine had been left there overnight in a hangar. On arrival, Wally and Bert wasted no time in getting aboard and checking everything out and then waited for it to get dark. With all of the preliminary checks out of the way, the fan duct motors were started and the Discovery taxied out of the hangar and stopped for a moment. After some final checks it ascended into the night sky, much to the amazement of the members of the Irish Air Corps stationed at the establishment who had come to watch.

Once the Discovery had reached 5,000 feet, Wally headed out to the Irish Sea before hovering and making a cloud. A Cumberland Grey makes a good imitation of a Scotch mist at ground level, commented Bert, and that's what they made. In the early hours of the morning, Wally took his Cumberland Grey to Dublin and on arrival overhead the city he descended to ground level to give it a taste of Scotch mist.

Early morning risers got a surprise when they opened their curtains and saw the Scotch mist, although more than likely they didn't know it was Scotch mist, unless they had attended the University lecture the night before. People struggled in the mist to get to work and buses made slow journeys. It was safer to walk in a Scotch mist but it still didn't prevent people going wrong and it wasn't long before Dublin was full of bad-tempered mist covered inhabitants.

Dublin got no relief as the Scotch mist hung around and tempers continued to fray. By midday those that had attended the University lecture wandered into what had been brought to Dublin. Some gathered samples in jam jars to take away for analysis whilst others used it as cover to carry out clandestine acts of aggression on vending machines.

Subjecting Dublin to a Scotch mist couldn't carry on, in spite of the strong affinity between Ireland and Scotland. It simply had to go. Folk had had enough of it and when word got out that students from the University had organised it there was hell to play. It didn't take long after that to get a message to Wally and it simply said in plain Irish – 'Bugger off and take your Scotch mist with you!'

Before lifting the Scotch mist off Dublin's fair city, Wally had a quick discussion with Bert. They now had a job at Kirkcudbright, raining on a parched farm, but after that they would head back to Wally's place in Cartmel for a few days instead of returning to Wythenshawe Weather Centre. They could put the Discovery down on the old airfield at Cark and leave it in a hangar there whilst they took time out. All that was required was a phone call to Wally's pal at Cark and it would all be settled. When this had been done, and much to the relief of Dublin, the mist lifted and drifted out to sea and one or two celebrations began but mostly in the University.

The Discovery settled at 5,000 feet and Wally punched the co-ordinates of his current location and those of his destination at Kirkcudbright into his soakometer/navaid and then put his feet up on the flight deck and left his machine to its own devices. He could view the open sky on his flight-deck TV screen and day dream about his dinky housemaid, a young lady by the name of Felicity. Bert, on the other hand, fell into a snooze. When all was said and done, his skipper could handle things on his own.

Travelling on a north-easterly heading, the crew of the Discovery was enjoying a relatively slow but smooth flight towards Galloway and Kirkcudbright. Whilst Bert snoozed, Wally marveled at the blue sky on his TV screen and the many beautiful clouds being propelled by a westerly wind. He was flying across the path of nature's work and it felt a bit eerie as the Discovery entered the confines of one of them and then emerged from the other side without having felt a thing. There was nothing new about this but Wally always marvelled at the experience.

The Nimbus, gracefully sailing on the air waves heading for Wythenshawe, was being carefully plotted on its journey by its crew. Cirrus divided his attention between his TV screen and his PPI whilst Puffy tracked the flight on a chart with the aid of the PPI. Although they were over the Irish Sea, the County Down coastline together with that of the Isle-of-Man was clearly depicted and this aided their navigation considerably. Little blips on the PPI identified aircraft in their locality. For the moment there was nothing in the locality that would require any adjustments to the flight path of the Nimbus.

Puffy turned from his chart table to view the sky's cavalcade on the flight-deck TV.

"Captain, don't you think the sky is such a beautiful place?"

"Yes I do. It's truly a wondrous place to be. We are so incredibly lucky."

"Is that Peel coming into view on the Isle-of-Man?" asked Puffy.

"Yes you're right, it is."

"It looks like we are converging with another cloud before we reach Peel, skipper."

"We'll pass straight through it just like all the others."

The Westmorland White surrounding the Nimbus entered the converging Cumberland Grey and its density reduced the visibility on the flight deck TV screen. That was just normal but it always induced a slight feeling of anxiety. It wouldn't last long, thought Cirrus, and it didn't. Suddenly there was a bang and a bump and the sound of grinding metal. The crew of the Nimbus was momentarily shocked and then the lights went out.

A drop in the sea

After the initial shock, Cirrus had the good sense to switch on the emergency power supply. He did this instinctively by groping in the dark for the panel of switches to the right of his cockpit seat. He had practiced for just this kind of event although he didn't know what this event actually was at this moment in time. He soon found what he was groping for and light was restored.

Both of the Nimbus crew quickly checked that they had suffered no injuries and then started to scan their own respective instruments to see if they could determine their situation. Cirrus could see that the Nimbus airspeed had dropped to zero which meant that any movement now would be determined by nature's wind. More importantly, he also observed from his altimeter that his machine was descending slowly. He concluded that the loss of forward movement meant that the Nimbus had lost its cloud buoyancy.

"Skipper, what's the score?"

"We are going down, Puffy. We are going to hit the sea."

"Crickey! You better deploy the parachutes."

"No I don't think so. They wouldn't work very well in our cloud and we are only descending slowly. I don't think there will be much of an impact."

Cirrus mused for a moment as the Nimbus continued its slow descent from 5,000 feet and then issued the instruction to Puffy to send out a 'May-Day' signal. He carefully read off the co-ordinates of their current position from his PPI. The message was sent out by Puffy using the recognised radio frequency dedicated to this purpose and he said a little prayer to himself at the same time – he wasn't a good swimmer.

"Puffy, you better get our life-jackets. We need to be prepared for when we hit the sea."

Cirrus looked above his head at the escape hatch and noted the position of the craft's flotation bag activation button. It was at this moment that he appreciated how useful the course he had recently done at the 'Guild of Cloud Owners' training centre at Bishops Court had been. It had given him a thorough insight into emergency procedures. His thoughts were interrupted by Puffy who had returned with the life-jackets.

"Shall we inflate them?" asked Puffy.

"No. Not until we know that we are going to have to use them," replied Cirrus.

With the altimeter showing the Nimbus down to 1,000 feet, Cirrus told his flight engineer that he would activate the flotation bags on impact and then open the escape hatch. They would both exit the craft's cockpit and sit and wait on the top of the fuselage.

When the impact came it was not severe and Cirrus carried out the drill he had planned. The crew clambered out of the craft and sat on its top in a mist; the Nimbus still had its Westmorland White creation. They could see that the flotation bags were keeping them afloat which was a great relief.

The roof of the Nimbus was slippery in the mist and Cirrus suggested that they inflate their life-jackets. If the craft rolled it would be easy to slip off. Being immersed in a mist meant that no-one could see them and so they activated the SARBE (Search and Rescue Beacon) attached to their life-jackets.

"That should help someone to find us, Puffy."

"Yeah and I hope the come bloomin quick, it's perishing damp and cool in a cloud!" he replied.

The Nimbus had come down on the sea just west of Peel and had attracted a good degree of interest from both the locals and its holidaymaker throng who had gathered in the harbour area to witness the event. Folk had heard a bang in the sky but couldn't see what it was and then, slowly, they could see a pearly white cloud descending towards the sea surface and another, which was greyer, apparently descending but continuing on a flight path that would bring it ashore, and there was rain coming from it.

"Well I never! I haven't seen anything like this before. Was it in the holiday brochure Bert?"

"I can't remember seeing anything Eth, but what's it all about?"

"Bless me! I haven't the foggiest."

"That's good Eth! You haven't the foggiest!"

And they both carried on watching the two mists descend until one of them sat on the surface of the sea and blotted out several boats in the process.

Rescuing a mist

The emergency services picked up the signal from the SARBE that both Cirrus and Puffy had activated and with the aid of the 'May-Day' message sent out, they were able to establish the position of the Nimbus which was offshore from Peel. Everything was being co-ordinated by the Air Rescue Co-ordination Centre at Kinloss in Scotland who were also aided by the local Police who were able to confirm that they had witnessed a cloud descending to sea level. The final piece in the search jig-saw was provided by the ID beacon onboard the cloud machine. The descending cloud that was being followed by a thousand eyes at Peel was indeed the cloud machine Nimbus.

The Police in Peel set about notifying the local lifeboat crew and within a relatively short time they mustered at the lifeboat station in the harbour. It didn't take the crew long to get launched and it was something exciting to watch. Few of the holidaymakers gathered on the seafront had ever witnessed the launching of a lifeboat and it would be something to tell everyone back at home.

The lifeboat picked up speed as it sailed out of Peel harbour and, once free of its restrictions it accelerated to a point were the bow lifted and a white wave trailed away on both the port and starboard sides to create a large 'v' shape in the sea. As it sped towards the mist, boats that it passed bobbed up and down on its bow wave and their crews gave waves to the lifeboatmen but they were not necessarily polite.

The lifeboat crew was a little mystified as to what they would find in the mist but they continued to head for it at high speed. As the mist got closer, the skipper gave the order to slow down and warned his crew to keep a sharp lookout once they entered it.

The skipper also knew that there were other boats in this mist and he gave the order to sound the fog-horn. The noise was tremendous and everyone immersed in the mist had no problem hearing it. In fact, it left them all momentarily deaf. For a few moments the skipper had a problem getting his crew to hear his next instruction which was to 'listen out'.

It felt strange onboard the lifeboat, creeping along in the thick mist to the accompaniment of the ripples of the sea down each side of the vessel. Each member strained to see through the mist and to hear any tell-tale sounds that might give them a clue as to the whereabouts of the hidden Nimbus. They did come close to a couple of fishing boats and it took a couple of swift evasive manoeuvres to avoid hitting them and a few unique fishing terms were exchanged.

The mist seemed to be getting thicker and the lifeboat was down to a crawl. Suddenly, and without any warning, the Nimbus appeared dead ahead, and before the skipper could slow down any further, there was a bump and a few expletives sailed out on the air-waves. Fortunately the impact was not too severe and other than a slight dent on the side of the Nimbus nothing else seemed to have happened. Momentarily the lifeboat crew could not make out the size or shape of the floating cloud machine but they could hear the welcome from its crew somewhere in the mist.

"You took your time. Where have you been all this time?" enquired Puffy

"What a greeting!" exclaimed the lifeboat skipper and the rest of his crew agreed.

Shortly after the impact, a breeze got up and the mist started to divorce itself from the Nimbus. It moved off towards Peel and started to ascend from sea level. Once freed from the weight of the Nimbus the mist crept higher to join nature's creations heading south-east on a north-westerly wind. Cirrus and Puffy were not used to being so visible and when they had lost their mist they felt quite naked. The lifeboat crew on the other hand marveled at what they were witnessing. After the initial surprise, the crew got down to business and the first thing they did was to rescue Cirrus and Puffy from the top of the fuselage and then the Nimbus was taken under tow to Peel.

Spectators in Peel couldn't believe their own eyes as they saw the lifeboat returning with what looked like a space-ship under tow and it had a dented nose.

"Have the Martians landed, Eth?" asked Bert.

"Are there any green men in the lifeboat?" replied Eth.

"Why do you ask that, Eth?"

"Well, I thought all Martians were green."

The lifeboat was now in Peel harbour and had come to a halt whilst the next action was considered. Cirrus and Puffy could overhear the conversation between Eth and Bert on the harbour quayside and Cirrus looked at Puffy.

"I thought we had left Ballyhalbert to get away from the Martians," remarked Puffy.

Cirrus just smiled and thought to himself how strange life can be.

Wet revenge

The Discovery was pushed eastwards by the impact of the colliding Nimbus and lost power at the same time. Any progress in a northerly direction came to a sudden halt. The shock of the collision threw Wally into a quandary but Bert was on the case.

"Wally, you better do something!"

After a few grunts and ahs, Wally came to the conclusion that they were in serious trouble and Bert better get a May-Day signal out at once.

The emergency services peered at their radar screens with greater scrutiny when the May-Day came in. They could be confident now that the unidentified blip they had been observing was indeed the Discovery. If it had had its ID beacon switched on its details would have appeared at the side of its radar blip and that would have removed totally any question about its identity. Nevertheless, they were confident that they were observing Wally's wonder machine and it was heading for the Manx coastline just north of Peel.

"Bert, I don't have any control of the Discovery and we are losing height and heading for the Manx mountains."

"What are we going to do then?" asked Bert.

"Well first, create a downpour and get rid of this dam cloud."

Bert faithfully complied and the Discovery crossed the coastline raining heavily on everything and everybody they happened to sail over.

"Cloud gone!" shouted Bert.

Free from his cloud, Wally could see through his cockpit window how low he was and the fast approaching mountains.

"Bert I'm going to deploy the parachutes. Strap in and hold tight; we're going to crash- land soon."

The Discovery came down in a field with a slight rise and the impact was not calamitous. Cows grazing in the field had a surprise but they soon returned to the business of grazing. Wally and Bert unstrapped and made their way to the exit door. Pushing the open button didn't get the entry door open and they had to use the manual lever to do the job. Once out on the ground, they both looked at the Discovery and were amazed at the large dent in the craft's port side.

"I wonder what did that?" asked Bert but Wally just scratched his head in disbelief.

Whilst the crew of the Discovery walked around their craft and inspected the damage, a very irate and very wet farmer made his way towards them. He was not pleased by his drenching and not pleased by the unexpected visitors in his field. He sought revenge, and his herd of cattle was taking a great interest in the goings on. Grazing became second priority.

Clearly the farmer had serious ideas relating to the general welfare of two astronauts that had dropped into his field without his permission and Wally and Bert began learning a new vocabulary.

Before things got really nasty, the emergency services arrived and through the field gate came a fire engine, an ambulance and two Police land-rovers and each left a clear imprint across the field, evidence of the route they had taken. Before the farmer could remonstrate with the latest arrivals, he spotted his herd of cattle vacating his field through an open gate and in sheer exasperation he left the scene to try and round them up before they went paddling.

Wally and Bert were both relieved that the emergency services had got to them before the farmer had.

Manx recovery

Almost within 24 hours of the cloud collision, engineers from Black, Black & Blackemore's had arrived on the island and immediately transported both the Nimbus and the Discovery to Jurby airfield. Ample hangar space was available there and the cloud machines could be kept out of the public eye.

Work began on both machines. It was relatively easy to replace the crunched nose on the Nimbus and it wasn't much more difficult to remove the dent on the port side of the Discovery, but it was a bit more complicated getting the electrics sorted and making the fan duct motors work again. Nevertheless, Black, Black & Blackemore's had engineers who had been in the business as man and boy and they knew all the ins and outs of it.

In the darkness of night each machine was wheeled outside its hangar and the engineers tested everything they could on the ground, and that included engine runs.

In no time at all the crews of the machines had the chance to get aboard their respective machines and give them a short flight around the Point-of-Ayr to check for themselves that everything functioned, and this was also done in the night-sky. When both crews were satisfied that the Nimbus and Discovery were fully operable they signed the engineer's clearance form and then it was a case of continuing the flight that had been interrupted by their collision.

Cirrus and Puffy headed for Wythenshawe Weather Centre and just managed to land and get inside its huge hangar before daybreak arrived. Mr.Spite was pleased to see them but had to break the news that the job in Somerset to get rid of a severe flood had gone to other cloud machine owners. Both crew members could fully understand that, considering that it was an emergency but, in the case of Puffy, it was partly alleviated when he caught sight of Goldilocks and he couldn't help smiling at her, but she didn't reciprocate. The crew headed back to the comfort of their Slaidburn home.

Wally and Bert continued their flight to the old airfield at Cark and, on arrival, the Discovery was taxied in to an old rusty looking hangar that was just big enough to take it, but that was fine as far as Wally was concerned. When the hangar doors were closed the two intrepid cloud men went their own ways, which in the case of Wally was to the lovely village of Cartmel. The thought of seeing Felicity again created a flood of tantalising images in Wally's mind and he was glad his mother wasn't living with him.

An enquiry

As with all aeronautical incidents, an enquiry was held to establish exactly what caused the collision between two cloud machines west of the Isle-of-Man. The enquiry was held at Wythenshawe Weather Centre and Mr I.N.Spite CDM was Head of the 'Enquiry Board'. Crews from both the Nimbus and the Discovery were summoned to attend along with certain members of the emergency services.

After rigorous questioning it was concluded that a number of factors had contributed to the Nimbus and Discovery colliding at 5,000 feet west, of Peel. A major factor had been the negligence shown by Mr Lenticular when he failed to switch on his ID beacon, thus preventing anyone plotting his course. Secondly, both crews had been negligent in not filing a flight plan before setting off on their respective flights. If they had, the authorities would have been aware of the potential hazard and got one of them to alter their altitude.

The Board determined that the major factor involved had been the woeful lack of attention paid by Mr Lenticular on what was going on around him. If he had not put his feet up on his flight-deck and daydreamed, he would have seen the Nimbus on his PPI and the information displayed would have clearly shown that he was on a collision path, being at the same altitude.

Wally was found guilty of flying without due care and attention and he got a penalty point on his pilot's licence. Both crews got a warning to be more diligent in the future but they both lived to rain on another day.

MARRYING UNDER A CLOUD

Unreasonable behaviour

The post had just been delivered to the Slaidburn home of the crew of the Nimbus and, as was usual practice, Puffy collected it from behind the front door. A quick scan through the small number of letters revealed an important looking envelope addressed to him. It had the words **'Strictly Confidential'** across the top in bold lettering.

Puffy scrambled to open the important looking letter whilst feeling a little apprehensive. It was unusual for him to receive anything labelled **'Strictly Confidential'** and in great anticipation he tore the envelope open. The letter came from a solicitor acting on behalf of his wife Carol. He read the contents carefully but before he could think much about it he was distracted by his skipper.

"Puffy, where is my morning cuppa? You're late this morning."

Puffy dutifully went about his business and took a cup of coffee and a copy of the Daily Gloom into the lounge where his boss, Cirrus, was sitting waiting. Cirrus was about to make a comment regarding the time but it was plainly observable from his companion's facial expression that all was not well.

"Is something the matter?" asked Cirrus.

"I have to go court, skipper."

"Whatever for?"

"Carol is suing me for a divorce."

Cirrus couldn't help thinking that a divorce was more than likely going to happen at some point but was flummoxed by the fact that Carol was suing Puffy.

"What grounds does she have to sue you for a divorce?"

"It's on the grounds of my unreasonable behaviour."

"What unreasonable behaviour?" asked a perplexed Cirrus.

"She doesn't say but she does cite Joanne Black as aiding and abetting me."

Apart from the fact that the grounds cited for the divorce were ridiculous it probably ended any chances of Puffy getting back with Joanne, or Goldilocks as she was known to everybody at Wythenshawe.

"I suggest you try contacting Goldilocks and seeing if she will discuss things with you."

"What good do you think that will do, skipper?"

"Well at least you can both present the same story in court," replied Cirrus.

Miss Joanne Black had also received a letter from Carol's solicitor and she was furious about it. The only involvement she had had with Percival White was a few dates. There had been no impropriety and what made her even more bad tempered was the fact that she hadn't known that he was married; at least that is what she had been telling herself. The truth of the matter was that nothing happened in Wythenshawe Weather Centre without word getting around. She had been aware that Puffy and Carol had got married but when they separated, and it happened several times, it was convenient to think of him as a single person. In spite of all this, she thought it was ludicrous that it was claimed that she had aided and abetted Puffy in his unreasonable behaviour towards Carol. Right now she wished she had never met Percival White.

The phone rang in Mr Spite's secretary's office and Joanne picked it up.

161

"Hello, Wythenshawe Weather Centre, Mr Spite's secretary speaking. How can I help you?"

"Hello Joanne!"

Miss Black could tell immediately that it was Puffy on the other end of the line but it was most unusual for him to address her by her real name. 'What's he after?' she thought.

"And what do you want, Mr White?" asked Joanne in a stern voice.

"I suppose you have had a letter from Carol's solicitor telling you that you are being cited in her divorce case?"

"Yes I have, and I'm not pleased about it."

"I can understand that and I think Carol is the one that's being unreasonable about things. Do you think we could meet and talk about things before the court hearing?"

"I don't think so, Puffy. It would be more appropriate if we kept apart before the court case."

With that, the phone went dead but Puffy felt that he had detected a slight change in attitude. Perhaps the damage could be repaired in the future.

The case begins

The divorce case was held in Bolton and it began with Carol White nee-Aspinall addressing the panel. She claimed that Percival had been conducting an affair whilst he was still married to her. When Joanne was called she presented a different story. She explained to the panel that Carol had left Percival on a number of occasions and indeed she was separated from him when Percival had dated her. There had been no impropriety and further to that it was also the case that Mrs White was indulging in affairs. The panel had to point out that it was not Mrs White who was currently being scrutinised and she was asked to step down.

Puffy said exactly the same thing to the panel as Joanne but not so eloquently, and then it was Carol who was cross-examined once more.

"Mrs White, are the panel correct in thinking that at the time you claim your husband was seeing Miss Black you were in fact separated from him?"

Carol coughed and spluttered before replying but admitted that that was the case.

"You can hardly describe your husband as being unreasonable if he was seeing Miss Black after you had left him."

Carol immediately realised that she was probably not going to win this case and resorted to using Puffy's excuse to house the two of them in a caravan. Once the panel had established that this was only to be a temporary arrangement until a barn had been converted into a new home, they dismissed the divorce case as without grounds. The marriage hadn't come to an end but at least the hearing had and Puffy's esteem had been improved.

With Carol's divorce petition quashed it left the door open for Puffy to file his own case on the grounds of desertion and his relationship with Goldilocks took a turn for the better.

Matrimonial moments

It wasn't long after Carol's abortive attempt to divorce Puffy before she got what she was after, but this time it was on his terms. She accepted that she had left him and it had all been due to the prospect of living with him in the confined space of a caravan with little or no chance of escaping from the stink of his feet. The latter point did not figure in the panel's deliberations and Mr Percival White was granted a divorce from Carol who would now be Carol Aspinall once again.

Relations between Goldilocks and Puffy improved once the divorce had been granted but that didn't stop her boss, Mr Spite, from questioning the wisdom of her getting in too deep. When all said and done, there was an age gap between the two of them. Nevertheless, their relationship blossomed and they both tried out each other's wrestling skills on several settees and enjoyed every moment.

It was inevitable that the question of marriage would come up at some time or another

And, when it did, the two cloud workers began by discussing where they would marry. Neither of them was particularly religious but a church in both Wythenshawe, where Goldilocks lived, and in Slaidburn, where Puffy lived, featured strongly in their thoughts. Even a church in Ballyhalbert came into the equation but it was eventually rejected as a candidate.

Musing things over one day in her office in Wythenshawe Weather Centre, Goldilocks was caught unawares as Mr Spite popped in.

"Good morning, Miss Black." Mr Spite did not approve of being over familiar with his secretary.

"You look deep in thought!"

"I can't decide where Puffy and I should get married."

Mr Spite was a little overcome by this revelation. Up until this point he had no idea they would be getting married. Before saying anything to his secretary he did a bit of musing himself.

"Can't you think of a nice church to perform the ceremony in?" he asked.

"We think a registrar would be more appropriate but we don't like the idea of a ceremony in a registrar's office," replied Miss Black.

"Then why don't you bring a registrar here?"

"Oh Mr Spite! You mean that Puffy and I could get married in the Weather Centre?"

"Exactly! You would be keeping it in the family, so to speak. You would be getting married under a cloud."

He wondered to himself how wise that last statement had been but it was too late now he had said it, but to make amends he made another suggestion.

"You could announce the wedding in 'The Monthly Downpour'.

Joanne was overcome with emotion at this point and embraced her boss and wept on his shoulder, and it was witnessed by his cleaner who had a more effective communication system than *'The Monthly Downpour'.*

The time came when it was necessary to talk about who would be the best man and who should give Goldilocks away. The choice of best man could only be Puffy's life-long skipper, Cirrus Cumulus, and when asked he was only too delighted to accept the invitation. The question of who should give the bride away was bit more complicated. Goldilocks' parents had passed away some years ago and she was an only child. She had to scrutinise the family photograph album to remind her who was left in her family. After several hours of painstaking scrutiny, she discovered that her late father's brother, Herbert, was still alive and living in Wythenshawe. She arranged to go and see him and when she did he gladly accepted the role in her marriage. Herbert was no stranger to giving things away; he had been doing it all his life and that was why he was almost penniless today.

Thoughts moved on to the subject of bridesmaids but after some debate Goldilocks decided that she didn't want any. Outside work she had few close friends and those she knew in work were more on a casual basis. The real point, however, was that she didn't want a lot of money to be spent on a wedding. Funds were needed for other more important things even if they were, in a sense, less romantic.

"Who are we going to invite to the wedding and where do you think we should have our reception?" asked Puffy.

These were two difficult questions but Mr Spite came to their rescue for a second time.

"Since you are going to announce the wedding in 'The Monthly Downpour', why not make your invitations through it as well?"

"That's a good idea but will all our guests be people that read it?" asked his secretary.

"Well I don't know where my parents live, so the only guests I would invite would be from the Weather Centre. What about you, Goldilocks?" asked Puffy.

After pausing for a moment she also felt that the only guests she would invite were also from Wythenshawe and she and Puffy agreed to start drawing up a list to place in the monthly journal.

"If all your guests are from here," said Mr Spite, *"why not have your reception in the The Silver Lining Club?"*

That made a lot of sense. Everything would be on one site, the wedding and the reception. Doing it this way would save a lot of money – no taxis and no invitation cards.

Things were going well and Mr Spite was flavour of the month.

"Phew, I will be glad when all this wedding stuff is done!" remarked Puffy.

"We want something to remember, don't we?" asked Carol. Not necessarily, thought Puffy, who remembered his last marriage, but right now wasn't the time to dwell on that.

"Is it all done now?"

"What about a honeymoon you old skinflint?" enquired Goldilocks.

Puffy scratched his head and several other parts of his anatomy but none of them created any inspiring ideas. He was at a loss.

Cirrus interrupted the couple and, having listened to their current dilemma, came up with a suggestion that they both grabbed with both hands.

"Why not go to Ballyhalbert?"

A new resident for Wythenshawe

The coming together of a Black and White would necessitate the search for a home sooner or later and it was getting later. Minds had been focussed on other things for some time but wrestling with each other on a settee was not going to solve the problem of where to live. It was a task that was beginning to take on some urgency.

Puffy loved the village of Slaidburn where he currently shared the 'Aurora Cloudealis' with his skipper, Cirrus. The house was fairly large and set in its own grounds. The whole village had an aura which Puffy loved to come back to after doing one of his many weather jobs. Goldilocks, on the other hand, lived in a high rise flat close to Wythenshawe's Weather Centre. She didn't drive and hence living close to the place she worked in was pretty handy. The nearest she came to the countryside was in the form of a flower-box on one of her windowsills.

Puffy was reluctant to leave his beloved village in the Bowland area of Lancashire but had to concede that unless Goldilocks was prepared to give up her current employment and look for a job near Slaidburn, in Clitheroe perhaps, he would have to move to Wythenshawe. After a somewhat heated debate, it became clear that Mr Spite's secretary clearly wanted to remain as Mr Spite's Secretary and there was only one thing for it and that was to find a place in Wythenshawe. The deal was more than sealed when she got him in an arm-lock and played on his cheek with her lips. Her enticing smell and close proximity overwhelmed Puffy and at that moment he couldn't help but surrender to her passion, and then they got back to arguing about where to live.

The two cloud workers embarked on a tour of local estate agents to find a potential home. It became abundantly clear at an early stage that most properties were simply too expensive. It was not just a case of finding the deposit but also the cost of the monthly mortgage payments. What they could afford looked a bit drab and when they arranged to view a few places they were not impressed. An additional problem they faced was their ability to find a mortgage lender. Puffy's income was not fixed. He didn't have a guaranteed amount of money coming in each month. The nature of his work was such that some months he rained a lot and some months represented a financial drought. Mortgage lenders were not impressed by this and lending had to be based on Goldilock's income which was not substantial. The couple began to despair a little at their predicament

Word got round the Weather Centre, well in fact it really got round *The Silver Lining Club*, and Guild members had some sympathy for the plight of the to-be-weds but that's where things stopped, at least for a while.

Ronnie Fog was due to retire; he had spent many years delivering weather solutions around the World and now it was time to take a well-earned rest. He was a local chap and had a house within five minutes walk of the Weather Centre. He had been thinking about selling his place but had not got round to putting it on the market yet. His first priority was to determine where he was going to go in his retirement. He had been lucky; a place had come available at The Guild's Grange-over-Sands rest home *'The Head in the Sky'* and Ronnie grabbed the opportunity with both hands. Being surrounded by folk he had something in common with appealed to him. When Ronnie got to hear that Puffy and Goldilocks were looking for a house, he decided to talk to them before putting his own place up for sale.

Puffy made it clear that he and Goldilocks were having a problem getting a mortgage but Ronnie told them not to bother. He was happy to agree a sale price and they could arrange to pay for it straight into his bank account each month, but he was happy for the monthly payments to vary according to how busy Puffy was with the weather. Ronnie even set an interest level well below that of the regular mortgage lenders.

Ronnie's place was a small detached house that needed a bit of work doing on it and it had a nice little garden. It was a great stroke of luck that Ronnie was retiring and prepared to sell his place at an affordable price, but that's just the kind of camaraderie that existed between members of 'The Guild of Cloud Owners' and Puffy and Goldilocks agreed to purchase it with gratitude.

The wedding was a great occasion with almost all of the Guild's members in attendance. Cirrus had done Puffy proud as his best man and Goldilocks' late father's brother, Herbert, gave her away in style. When the registrar had done her bit, the assembled guests made their short way to *The Silver Lining Club* for the reception. A good meal was had by everyone and with the speeches done it was down to the serious business of dancing and boozing, although boozing was probably slightly ahead in the early stages. There was even a group of cloud workers that attempted to do the 'Stormbart Slow Stomp' but they were not graceful and lacked co-ordination but no-one minded.

A week in Ballyhalbert was bliss for the newlyweds who were both disappointed when it was time to return but, as always, all good things come to an end eventually and work and earning money beckoned. There was a mortgage to pay now.

A quiet house in Slaidburn

The Nimbus was between jobs and its skipper, Cirrus Cumulus, was resting in his Slaidburn home. He now had to fend for himself and it all felt a bit strange. He had had to nip down to the village shop to get a copy of the Daily Gloom and when he got back he had to make his own cup of coffee. He could cope with all this but he did miss Puffy calling in on him and then having an opportunity to tell him how the country was being mis-run. It was all too quiet.

What with Puffy's divorce, followed by a house search in Wythenshawe and then a wedding, it had been very hectic and now there was nothing happening. Life without his life-long colleague and faithful friend was suddenly a reality and Cirrus didn't much care for it. It wasn't the only thing Cirrus didn't care for. He wasn't keen on a whole range of domestic jobs that his companion had done for him: cooking, shopping, washing clothes and ironing, none of them inspired him. It was all going to get very tedious.

Captain Cirrus Cumulus had firmly reached the conclusion that he did not like peace. He desperately needed someone that he could complain to about the way the world was; he needed to say how he would put the world to rights. He had tried this in the village pub but it wasn't the place for serious ear-bashing. Drinkers simply turned away and talked about football or the new barmaid who was getting more attractive as each pint was drunk.

Maybe a housemaid would be an answer to the dilemma that Cirrus was currently faced with, but a housemaid was not the same as a colleague. It was after contemplating about a housemaid that Cirrus began to turn his thoughts to Abigail. She had always been apprehensive about coming between Cirrus and Puffy but that would not be the case now – there was no Puffy around. Perhaps it was time for him to seek his desires; perhaps he should reconsider proposing to her. Maybe he ought to locate that ring he had purchased some time ago.

The phone rang out and a very feminine voice answered.

"Hello, Cirrus. How are you coping without Puffy being around?"

"Hello, Abigail. I'm not coping. I can't stand all this peace and quiet."

"It's early days yet, Cirrus. You will get used to it."

"The truth is, Abigail, I don't want to get used to it. Do you think you could get over to my place for a few days? I want to ask you something."

The line went quiet for a few moments and then Abigail spoke again.

"I would be glad to. When shall I come?"

"Can you make it today?"

"You are in a hurry. Ok. I'll be with you in a couple of hours."

Abigail had been half expecting Cirrus to call her. Now that Puffy had left things were different. Maybe it was time for a change in her life.

The sound of Abigail's car on the gravel drive announced her speedy arrival and it was music to the ears of Cirrus. Greeting her at the front door he was delighted to see her. She looked very smart and fresh-faced. In fact she looked adorable and whilst he wanted to embrace her he couldn't muster the courage, but Abigail did it for him and he felt ecstatic. She felt good and smelled good.

Cirrus decided that they would stroll down to the 'Hark-to-Bounty' pub for a meal rather than try out his primitive cooking skills on her. He had been known to burn water and had a reputation for double-sided black toast. The atmosphere in the pub was homely and the meal was very tasty. A number of Cirrus's acquaintances were a little taken aback by the obvious warmth between the two cloud workers and it became an intriguing point of conversation but no-one interrupted the couple. Clearly there was romance in the air.

Returning arm in arm to the Cumulus residence, Abigail looked at the name that Cirrus and Puffy had given it – 'Aurora Cloudealis'- it was so colourful, she thought. The two of them settled in the lounge and Cirrus appeared to take a small box out of a drawer. He sat down to face Abigail and looked quite serious. Several moments passed and he didn't say a thing. Abigail had to break the deadlock.

"Is there something you want to ask me, Cirrus?"

Cirrus opened the little box that he had taken from the drawer to reveal a ring.

"Abigail, will you marry me?"

A uniting of clouds

Word got round fast in Wythenshawe and it wasn't long before Cirrus and Abigail received congratulatory messages from their many friends and colleagues who had all been wondering how long it would take before they took this step. The two of them were so well liked and respected at the Weather Centre that the 'Guild of Cloud Owners' placed a special announcement in the next edition of 'The Monthly Downpour' to ensure that none of its membership were left in the dark.

Both Abigail and Cirrus got on with discussing a wedding soon after he had proposed to her. Neither of them had any desire to have a long engagement and thoughts turned to where they should get married. Clitheroe and Slaidburn were the first two locations to spring to mind! Clitheroe was

Abigail's home town; indeed, she currently shared her family home there with her sister Lucy. The Windrush sisters' parents had bequeathed the house to their two daughters. George Windrush had passed away several years previously whilst mother, Ethel, who was frail and suffering from senile dementia, was cared for in a local residential home. Since both sisters were employed in a line of business that was unpredictable and forced them to spend frequent periods of time away from Clitheroe, a residential home for mum had been the only practical solution. The need to have a wedding in Clitheroe was not, given Abigail's circumstances, necessarily the only choice.

Abigail had been christened in Clitheroe's St.Mary Magdelene C-of-E Church, as had her sister Lucy, and naturally this did figure in the planning of where to get married. It was also remembered that this was the church at which Cirrus had brought the Nimbus to fulfill a revenge drenching of a wedding party some years earlier, but the least thought about that now the better. Slaidburn also had a very charismatic and oldy-world church which should be considered. The Parish Church of St.Andrews had a very special feel about and it reeked of history. It was in a charming location and its very English character appealed to Cirrus.

Thoughts turned to other possible locations and they included Ballyhalbert, where Cirrus had his second home. He loved to escape here after a particularly arduous weather job but he was less well versed in its religious establishments. It was during the consideration of Ballyhalbert as a wedding location that Abigail raised an interesting idea.

"You know, Cirrus, I rather liked that little church near Portaferry."

"You mean Ardquin Parish Church?"

"Yes that's the one. I remember Al Blighty's funeral service being held there."

"That was a special occasion. I remember it well."

Cirrus and Abigail mused for some time but in the end they both agreed, Ardquin Parish Church it was to be and they set about contacting the vicar and setting a date.

Who should be invited was quite a simple task for the two cloud workers. It was, simply, all of their colleagues, and Mr Spite was happy to announce the wedding and invites in 'The Monthly Downpour' which seemed to be including these kinds of announcements on something of a regular basis these days. All those who wished to attend the wedding would be given time off from delivering weather solutions and whilst their machines were parked in Wythenshawe's huge hangar they could take a more conventional flight to Northern Ireland for the great event.

"Cirrus, where do you think we should have our reception?"

"Do you remember where we went after Al Blighty's funeral?"

"Ah yes, I do! It was an hotel run by Al's brother, Sean and his sister, Maureen. Now let me think, it was called 'The Blight on the Shore.'

"That's the one. What about booking that for the reception?"

Plans were coming together now and not much was left to sort out. The church had been booked and a vicar found to perform the marriage ceremony and Sean and Maureen had been delighted to be asked to provide the reception, but what about a best man and bridesmaids? Neither provided any headaches. Abigail's sister would be a bridesmaid and the composer, Lucy Pankhurst, a friend of both of them, would be the other. Lucy P, which is how she was usually referred to, to avoid confusion, had composed the piece 'St.Kilda's Fling' which had been played in a concert held onboard a cruise liner in Village Bay, on the island of St.Kilda, a couple of years ago. The best man could only be Puffy but it was thought to be more appropriate for him to become Percival White, at least for the duration of the wedding.

A more delicate problem was who should give Abigail away? When word got around, as it did with most things at Wythenshawe, nods and winks were made in Mr Spite's direction and when he offered his services in a most diplomatic way, he was accepted most graciously. Indeed, behind the scenes, both Cirrus and Abigail were immensely flattered that Mr Spite CDM was going to do it; it was a great honour.

In the confines of his office in Wythenshawe Weather Centre, Mr Spite had been secretly thinking about some honeymoon plans for two of his favourite cloud workers.

"Miss Black, could you bring me that file on the 'Gondalus' please?"

Miss Black, or Goldilocks as she was known to most of the cloud fraternity, wiggled in her usual way as she entered Mr Spite's office but it didn't make much of an impression on him. She laid the file on his desk and wiggled out of his office, and again it didn't make any impression.

The cloud machine 'Gondalus' had been mothballed at the back of Wythenshawe's hangar ever since it was used on a cruise around Scotland by a couple from the USA. It didn't seem to have much of a future but it just might have one more important role to play. The top deck had been fitted out as a lovers' luxurious cruise cabin by the manufacturer, 'Black,Black & Blackemores in deeper Salford. Mr Spite contacted Cirrus's friend, Wally Lenticular, and together they inspected the 'Gondalus' at the back of the hangar and both agreed that it was in pretty good shape. If the engineers could give the craft a checking over and if a volunteer crew and a chef could be found then, hey presto, a honeymoon cruise could be laid on by 'The Guild' and that really would be something special. It was all duly organised in great secrecy but someone still managed to attach some large 'L' plates on it.

A smelly problem

A knock on the front door disturbed the slumber that Cirrus was enjoying and, once wakened, he made his way to see who it was. When he opened the door he got a pleasant surprise. Standing there with a suitcase in each hand was his faithful flight engineer, Puffy, and he didn't look too happy.

"Come in, come in. What brings you here? I wasn't expecting you."

"I didn't expect to be coming," replied a despondent Puffy.

Cirrus led his colleague into the lounge and sat him down. Before beginning any lengthy conversation he suggested he make them both a coffee and with Puffy's nod of agreement he rushed off to make it.

"What's happened? Something clearly has."

"She's kicked me out!"

"Why on earth has she done that?"

"Goldie has the most supernatural odour detectors."

Cirrus was puzzled by this and it showed on his face.

"It's my feet. Goldie says they stink."

Cirrus was aware that Puffy's feet were not one of his best assets. Over the years he had grown accustomed to the odour they generated and he had adapted by taking certain precautionary measures.

Puffy went on to explain that Goldilocks couldn't cope with his odours and had given him his marching orders, odours included.

The story continued to unravel as Puffy explained how it was customary for him at the end of a long, laborious cold job, to get into bed with his socks on. Goldilocks became aware of his arrival by virtue of her super-sensitive nostrils and nausea usually followed. Broken nights on a fairly regular basis, coupled with foot stench, are not ingredients that foster good relationships and short of having his feet amputated there was not going to be any easy solution. There may have been a simpler way of dealing with the problem but currently it escaped both of them.

No marriage can be sustained with smelly feet and Puffy's were no exception. Goldilocks had a delicate odour threshold and once exceeded there was no way she could be placated. He simply had to take his odour generators somewhere else and here he was, back at Cirrus's Slaidburn home.

"Well I am sorry to hear this, Puffy, but you know you will always have a place here."

Having said that, Cirrus suddenly became aware of what had upset Goldilocks so much; his nostrils were beginning to twitch. He really hadn't got round to thinking about any other ramifications at this point

Puffy needed to get things off his chest and the tale of his woes continued.

"I can't understand why my feet were such a problem."

"What makes you say that?"

"Well, most of my work is done in the night whilst Goldie is sleeping. When she works, I'm sleeping. We only slept together on odd occasions. I even tried sleeping in another room but she still complained about the odour. She said it came under the bedroom door and up the walls."

Cirrus scratched his head for inspiration but all he got was a bit of dandruff, so he kept scratching and just listened.

"She followed me around everywhere with an air-freshener. It got to a stage were she wouldn't wash my socks; in fact she wouldn't even touch them. I ended up buying new socks by the millions."

"Come on Puffy, you're exaggerating."

"Skipper, I tell you, I tried to get into the habit of always taking my socks off before getting into bed but it made no difference."

"Where did you put the socks you had taken off?"

"I put them in my shoes at the side of the bed which is where I always leave the shoes I have just stepped out of."

Cirrus couldn't help thinking to himself how inept Puffy could be. He could imagine the odour from his socks rising from his shoes and slowly wafting past his wife's delicate nostrils. It must have been a very distressing sensation.

"You know, Skipper, the final straw came when she burned my favourite shoes and here I am."

You may be here now Puffy, thought Cirrus, but right now you are a smelly cat amongst the pigeons.

Another unexpected crisis

Bernard Thrift had something in common with Puffy, namely socks. He had made a vast fortune out of manufacturing socks. His socks had a foothold on every continent on the planet. His socks covered literally millions of feet everyday all around the world and brought him satisfaction and loads of money. His success had been achieved by manufacturing odour-free socks. The most pungent feet in the world could not be detected in a pair of his socks but it is unknown whether Puffy had tried them. Thrifty socks were available in almost every country and currently sales were breaking records in places like India and China, and Bernard was getting letters to thank him from thousands of grateful wives. There was no doubt that Thrifty socks were making a wonderful contribution to a foot-odour-free world but there were still a few million feet to go, especially in places like India and China and, to a lesser extent, Wythenshawe.

Every year, Bernard Thrift was faced with a huge tax demand on his company profits. He didn't object to making a contribution towards the well being of his native country. He was to an extent a patriot. What he did object to was the way in which the Government spent a high proportion of its tax income. He was opposed to many of the things that his tax money was spent on and had little regard for the values or opinions of politicians. It seemed to him that the tax contributions he was making were being largely wasted and he made it a mission to put his company's profits out of reach of the Inland Revenue.

The Isle-of-Man and The Channel Islands had been used by some as a kind of tax haven and monies invested there had been outside the grasp of the UK Government. Bernard, on the advice of his finance controller, had taken advantage of this situation and successfully avoided paying what he considered as excess taxation by using what the Isle-of-Man had to offer. When he read in his newspaper about Government spending he had no doubts that he was doing the right thing. As far as he was concerned, the Government could pour money away in whatever frivolous way it wished as long as it was not his well-earned cash.

The UK Government had been aware for some time that various companies and individuals were effectively using tax havens to avoid paying tax, and various agreements with places like the Isle-of-Man and the Channel Islands appeared to legalise it but it was still considered as tax evasion, clever though it was. There were even individuals in these places who doubted the morality of what they were complicit in but it did help their own economies and that removed any pressure to change. Money was more potent than morality.

There had been considerable debate amongst the UK's political class to get rid of this tax evasion loophole for some time and eventually discussions took place between all the interested parties, excluding of course the tax evaders. Eventually, the Manx Government entered into an agreement with the UK Government and its tax haven status rapidly evaporated along with loads of Bernard Thrift's fortune. It was no consolation to learn that other individuals had been affected in the same way. All Bernard could see was a large chunk of his hard-earned money being swallowed up by the Inland Revenue.

Bernard's ego took a dive and he hated the Isle-of-Man for it with a vengeance. He hated the lump it was in the middle of the Irish Sea; he hated everyone that lived on the island. In spite of his feelings being somewhat irrational, he could not bring himself around to forgiving them. As he sat looking at his tax demand from the Inland Revenue, his vengeance increased and he vowed that the Isle-of-Man was going to pay. He would make them pay for aiding and abetting the UK Government.

It took some time for the Head of 'Thrifty Socks' to work out what he was going to inflict on the Isle-of-Man but he got there in the end. Discussions with a large wind farm manufacturer resulted in him engaging the company in a secret deal. Work began off the Cumbria coast just outside territorial waters and large consignments of wind farm equipment was shipped to the area. There was considerable interest amongst those who witnessed the comings and goings of well laden ships but no-one seemed to have any knowledge regarding what was going on. Most of the work went on under the cover of darkness. Only the powerful arc lights aboard the ships involved were used as the secret work progressed.

Bernard Thrift had embarked on a huge engineering project. He was about to do something that had never been done before and he couldn't afford to rush things. It was a wonder that he could afford to pay for it all but he was a billionaire. There are a lot of feet in the world to put socks on and especially in India and China and, to a lesser extent, in Wythenshawe.

Slowly but surely the project was nearing completion and soon it would be time to go and view what had been done in the Irish Sea off the Cumbria Coast. Bernard was ferried out to the HQ vessel upon which he was introduced to the principal engineer behind it all. A cabin had been set aside onboard the ship to showcase the work achieved. In the room on a large table a map was spread out which illustrated the sea bed in the area, and the position of a wind farm on the sea bed was highlighted. It was most impressive and certainly unique but it left a lot to the imagination. The project head drew Bernard's attention to a large TV screen that had been mounted on the cabin wall and, operating a hand held remote control he brought the screen to life. A very clear image of the sea bed could be perceived and there was the sea bed wind farm in all its glory.

Mr Thrift was informed that all that was now required was a test run and it was agreed to initiate this in the next few days. In the next 48 hours a ship with a diesel-driven electrical generator aboard arrived on the scene and engineers coupled a large cable from the underwater sea bed to the ship's generator output. The first test was to be conducted in the early hours of morning and observers were placed on the Cumbria coast. At an agreed time, power was applied to the underwater wind farm and a dozen huge propellers began to slowly rotate and a wave of growing height was spotted on the surface of the sea heading in the direction of the Cumbria coast. As the wind propellers continued to rotate, the wave got bigger and travelled further until it finally spent itself on the coast. The test was regarded as successful and the mathematicians onboard gleaned enough information to allow them to calculate what speed they needed the propellers to rotate at and for how long.

For the next test two small fishing boats with observers aboard were sent out in an area to the west of the floating power station and using GPS, they accurately positioned themselves at fixed distances between the Isle-of-Man and the underwater wind farm. Whilst this was going on, the propeller blades on each wind generator on the sea bed were rotated through 180°. Darkness arrived and time slowly passed before the order was finally given to switch on the wind farm. As for the previous test, it wasn't long before a wave could be observed in the arc light and it was moving across the surface of the Irish Sea in the desired direction.

The crew onboard the first observers' boat could make out the approaching wave as it neared the vessel. It didn't looking menacing although its impact lifted the craft several feet up. The second observers' boat hardly noticed anything; the generated wave had largely petered out by the time it had reached it, in fact it was little different from the existing sea swell. Radio messages passed back and forth between the observers' boats and the floating power station, and different trials were held using different propeller rotation speeds for different lengths of time, until the principal engineer had all the data he required.

That was a great relief for the shipping in the area who, for the last few hours had been wondering what the devil was going on. One wave after another had lifted them in the water and each had been bigger than the last. The confusing thing was that the intervals between them seemed to vary; there was no consistent pattern to what they were experiencing. To cap it all off, the last wave was astronomical and it took some time to scrape stuff off galley walls as well as bits of kit getting washed overboard. There had been no indication in the weather forecast that this was going to happen.

Now it was down to Bernard. It was his decision and his alone. The vast amount of money he had invested in getting his own back would be unleashed whenever he desired and for the moment he gloated on what had been achieved and what he was about to unleash. There was no hurry involved, just gloating, and all provided by the sock-purchasing public around the world but mostly in India and China and, to a lesser degree, in Wythenshawe.

Wythenshawe supreme

The alarm bells sounded in Wythenshawe Weather Centre and the emergency operations room was activated to deal with the incoming catastrophe. Mr Spite had taken command and with his designated emergency team he convened a meeting to establish the nature of what had happened before determining how the Guild's members should act.

A tsunami size wave had hit the east coast of the Isle-of-Man in the early hours of the morning and flooded all the low lying coastal regions. There had been an exodus of people from villages and towns affected and everyone had headed for the slopes of the island's main mountain, Snae Fell. They were all in a pretty desperate state and hyporthermia was a strong possibility if aid didn't get to them quickly. It would not be possible to go back to their homes as long as the flooding persisted and the prospect of a cold night on the mountainside without any warm clothing was nothing to look forward to.

The emergency team had to consider what aid they could give and then get on with it and fast. Supplying food and blankets was the province of other sectors of the emergency services. The unique skill that Wythenshawe could bring to the scenario was the ability to remove the flood waters. The team only had an estimate of the amount of flood water and they were unaware of whether there would be any further huge waves of sea water. It was, however, concluded that they needed to get as many cloud machines as possible to the scene and get them to atomise the flood water and take it in cloud form somewhere else and rain it off.

The Centre's situation report board was scrutinised to see who was available. It was fortunate for the Isle-of-Man that most members were not currently tasked; they were all about to attend the imminent marriage of Cirrus Cumulus to Abigail Windrush. This was to the advantage of the Isle-of-Man but less so for the wedding couple.

The phone rang in the Ballyhalbert residence of Cirrus and he was most disturbed by the news that greeted him.

"You mean I have to drop everything and get back to Wythenshawe?"

"I'm afraid that's the top and bottom of it, Cirrus. I am so sorry to do this almost on the eve of your wedding but we do have a duty to those folk on the Isle-of-Man."

Cirrus couldn't argue with this but was deeply saddened all the same. His wedding should be taking place in 48 hours time. What would Abigail think about all this?

Before he could do anything else the phone rang again and it was Abigail and she sounded as if she was crying. That struck home hard. Cirrus had never heard Abigail cry before and he didn't enjoy it. When she did speak she was immensely positive and seemed to brush the whole thing to one side.

"I suppose we'd better get our machines up and away and get on with the relief operation, Cirrus. We will just have to postpone the wedding until a later date but it can't be helped."

What a wonderful attitude to have, thought Cirrus, and he started to pack.

Government clampdown on reporting

A rumour was spreading that the Isle-of-Man had experienced a tsunami and people living in coastal areas around the UK were beginning to panic. Until it was possible to establish the true nature of what the island had experienced, the Government, in its infinite wisdom, placed a ban on all reporting of information relating to the matter.

As a result of the Government ban, it has not been possible to clarify either the outcome of the relief operation or the results of the investigation into what the Manx population had experienced.

What can be reported is that the 'Gondalus' was put back in mothballs and the marriage between Abigail Windrush and Cirrus Cumulus was put on hold until a more opportune time. It's a sad business but just another indication of the way in which the weather influences all our lives.

EPILOGUE

So many unanswered questions

The imposition of a reporting ban on the Manx crisis has made it impossible to get to the bottom of what exactly was going on and that's particularly frustrating when you already know so much, but presumably, it will all come out in the wash eventually.

You will have arrived here with so many unanswered questions. How did the flood relief operation go on the Isle-of-Man? Did Bert Thrift get caught for generating the tsunami that caused Manx chaos? Did Cirrus and Abigail eventually tie the knot?

Did Puffy and his smelly socks get reconciled with Goldilocks?

I know as much about these things as you do, so don't ask me! Anyway, I'm busy sorting out my own smelly feet problem. Now where did I put those odour eaters?

ABOUT THE AUTHOR

This is the fourth book about weather solutions by the author, the first being – 'Making Rain and Other Things Is Our Business!', the second – 'A Cloud's Life' and the third – 'Weather to Order'.

Tony Smith is a retired Further Education Lecturer and former RAFVR(T) and SCC RNR Officer. He has a wealth of experience of young people and all things flying. As a Bachelor of Education and glider pilot, he is suitably qualified to waffle on about a lot of things.

When Tony's head is not in the clouds he builds model aircraft and helps a local Brass band.

Tony is married and has two daughters, two granddaughters and a grandson. He lives in Atherton, a former mining and mill town in the north-west of England.

The Author, on the right, seeking spiritual cloud guidance from
Rev. Raymond Cooke on the Quarterdeck at SCTC Inskip.

Illustrations

Illustration one

Manufacturers – Black, Black & Blackemore's, Salford

Cloud Machine – Nimbus – grade 1

SIDE ELEVATION

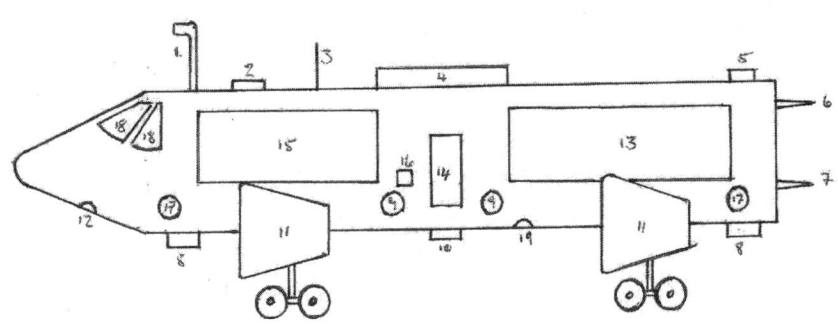

1. Periscope with tv camera which has infra-red capability to see through cloud or in the dark.
2. GPS antennae (Global Positioning System).
3. VSI antennae (Vertical Separation Indicator – used in cloud formation flying).
4. Emergency parachutes.
5. Identification Beacon (every cloud machine has its own ID code)
6. Telephone antennae.
7. Radio Transmitter/Receiver antennae.
8. Atomiser – converts water into cloud by a process of evaporation (some water is stored onboard, some as ice).
9. Dispenser – converts stored water and stored ice plus cloud vapour into rain by a process of melting and condensing.
10. SOAKometer – early form of navigation aid with built in water location system.
11. Fan Duct Motor – propels cloud. A cloud has its own natural buoyancy.
12. Porthole for winch cable.
13. Saddle type water storage tank.
14. Side entry door.
15. Fuel tank for Fan Duct Motors.
16. Panel of buttons to open/close entry door and deploy/retract entry ladders.
17. Loudpeakers.
18. Cockpit window.
19. Fuel hose point.

Illustration two

<u>Manufacturers – Black, Black & Blackemore's, Salford</u>

<u>Cloud Machine – Nimbus – grade 1</u>

<u>PLAN VIEW</u>

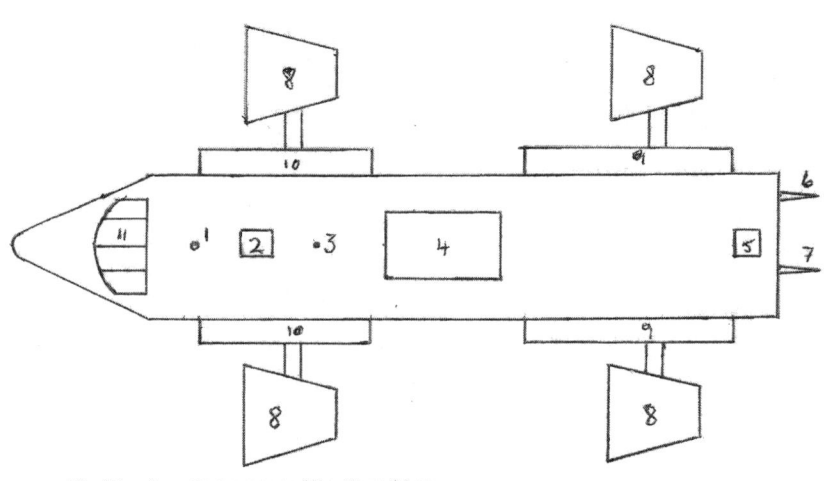

Direction of movement of Fan Duct Motors
to yaw the cloud left or right.
Movement made by cockpit rudder pedals.

1. Periscope with tv camera which has infra-red capability to see through cloud or in the dark.
2. GPS antennae (Global Positioning System).
3. VSI antennae (Vertical Separation Indicator – used in cloud formation flying).
4. Emergency parachutes.
5. Identification Beacon (every cloud machine has its own ID code)
6. Telephone antennae.
7. Radio Transmitter/Receiver antennae.
8. Fan Duct Motor – propels cloud. A cloud has its own natural buoyancy.
9. Saddle type water storage tank..
10. Fuel tank for Fan Duct Motors.
11. Cockpit window.

Illustration three

Manufacturers – Black, Black & Blackemore's, Salford

Cloud Machine – Nimbus – grade 1

FRONT VIEW

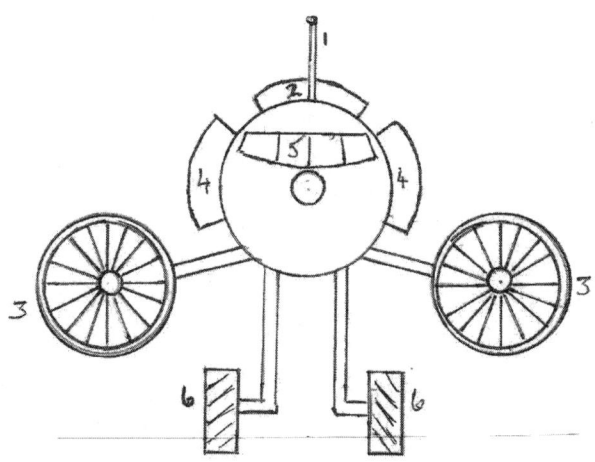

1. Periscope with tv camera which has infra-red capability to see through cloud or in the dark.
2. Emergency parachutes.
3. Fan Duct Motor – propels cloud. A cloud has its own natural buoyancy.
4. Fuel tank for Fan Duct Motors.
5. Cockpit window.
6. Rugged undercarriage.

Illustration four

Manufacturers – Black, Black & Blackemore's, Salford

Cloud Machine – Nimbus – grade 1

GENERAL ARRANGEMENTS

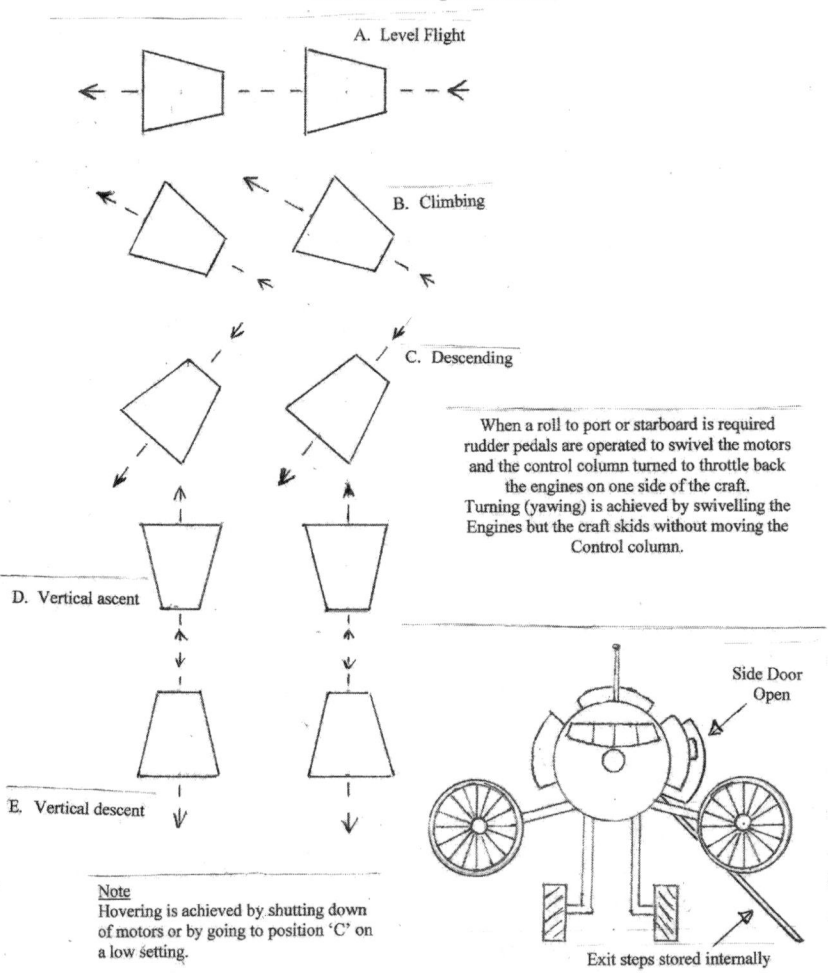

Fan Duct Motors (port side shown)

A. Level Flight

B. Climbing

C. Descending

When a roll to port or starboard is required rudder pedals are operated to swivel the motors and the control column turned to throttle back the engines on one side of the craft.
Turning (yawing) is achieved by swivelling the Engines but the craft skids without moving the Control column.

D. Vertical ascent

E. Vertical descent

Side Door Open

Note
Hovering is achieved by shutting down of motors or by going to position 'C' on a low setting.

Exit steps stored internally

192

Illustration five

Manufacturers – Black, Black & Blackemore's, Salford

Cloud Machine – Nimbus – grade 1

INTERNAL LAYOUT

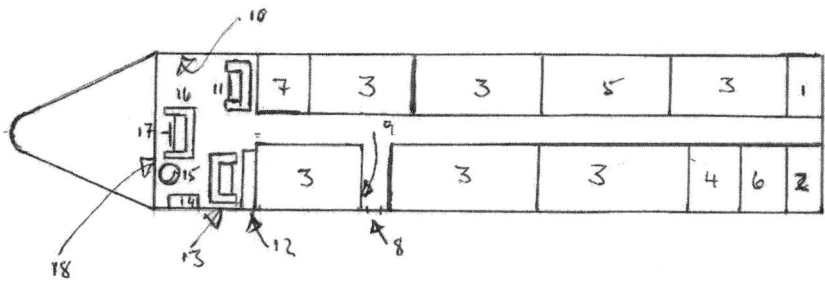

1. Wash room.
2. Toilet
3. Refrigerator.
4. Mixer.
5. Sublimator.
6. Van de Graaf Generator.
7. Galley.
8. Side entry door.
9. Panel of buttons.
10. Drop down bunk location.
11. Passenger seat.
12. Flight Engineer's station.
13. Flight engineer's seat.
14. Winch winding mechanism.
15. Plan Position Indicater.
16. Pilot's seat.
17. Control column.
18. Flight deck instrument panel.

Illustration six

**PILOT'S COCKPIT
ARRANGEMENTS**

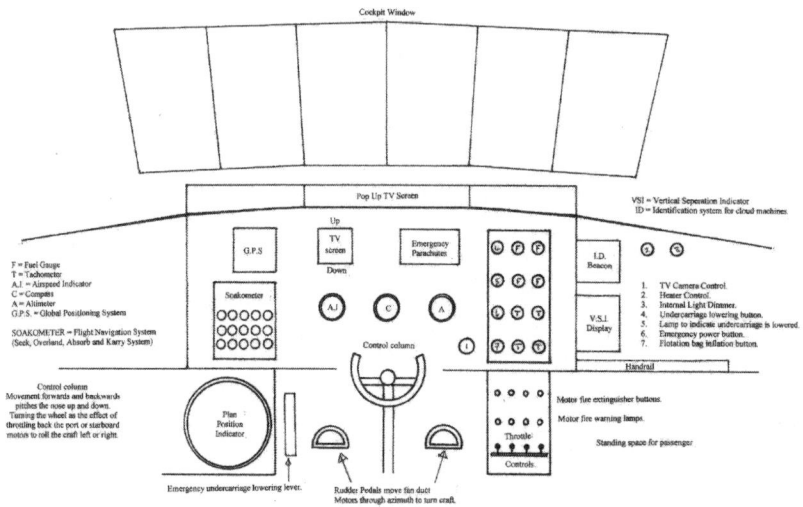

Cockpit Window

Pop Up TV Screen

VSI = Vertical Seperation Indicator
ID = Identification system for cloud machines

F = Fuel Gauge
T = Tachometer
A.I = Airspeed Indicator
C = Compass
A = Altimeter
G.P.S. = Global Positioning System

SOAKOMETER = Flight Navigation System
(Seek, Overland, Absorb and Karry System)

Control column
Movement forwards and backwards
pitches the nose up and down.
Turning the wheel as the effect of
throttling back the port or starboard
motors to roll the craft left or right.

G.P.S

TV screen

Up

Down

Emergency
Parachutes

Soakometer

AI   C   A

Control column

I.D.
Beacon

V.S.I.
Display

1.   TV Camera Control.
2.   Heater Control.
3.   Internal Light Dimmer.
4.   Undercarriage lowering button.
5.   Lamp to indicate undercarriage is lowered.
6.   Emergency power button.
7.   Flotation bag inflation button.

Handrail

Plan
Position
Indicator

Emergency undercarriage lowering lever.

Rudder Pedals move fan duct
Motors through azimuth to turn craft.

Motor fire extinguisher buttons.

Motor fire warning lamps.

Throttle
Controls

Standing space for passenger

Illustration seven

Cloud Machine – Nimbus – grade 1

Manufacturers – Black, Black & Blackemore's, Salford

Flight Engineers Station

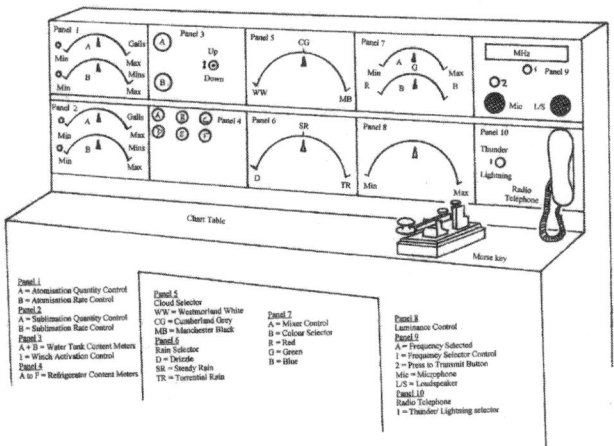

Panel 1
A = Atomisation Quantity Control
B = Atomisation Rate Control
Panel 2
A = Sublimation Quantity Control
B = Sublimation Rate Control
Panel 3
A + B = Water Tank Content Meters
1 = Winch Activation Control
Panel 4
A to F = Refrigerator Content Meters

Panel 5
Cloud Selector
WW = Westmorland White
CG = Cumberland Grey
MB = Manchester Black
Panel 6
Rain Selector
D = Drizzle
SR = Steady Rain
TR = Torrential Rain

Panel 7
A = Mixer Control
B = Colour Selector
R = Red
G = Green
B = Blue

Panel 8
Luminance Control
Panel 9
A = Frequency Selected
1 = Frequency Selector Control
2 = Press to Transmit Button
Mic = Microphone
L/S = Loudspeaker
Panel 10
Radio Telephone
1 = Thunder/ Lightning selector

Illustration eight

<u>Manufacturers – Black, Black & Blackemore's, Salford</u>

<u>Cloudtanic later renamed Gondalus</u>

<u>FRONT VIEW</u>

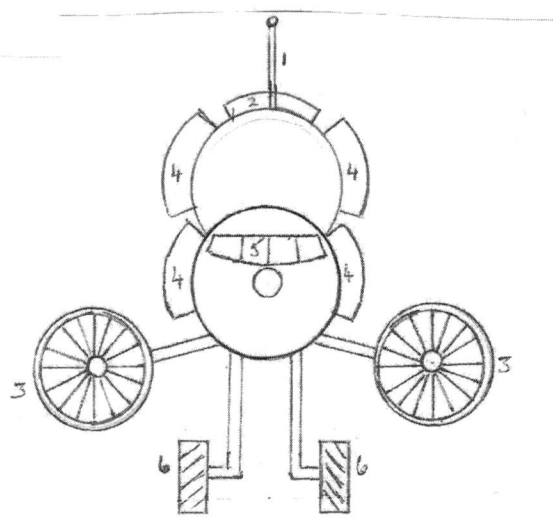

1. Periscope with TV camera with infra-red capability to see through cloud or in the dark.
2. Emergency parachutes.
3. Fan Duct Motor – propels cloud.
4. Fuel tank for Fan Duct Motors. Extra water tanks fitted behind these tanks.
5. Cockpit window.
6. Rugged undercarriage.

Illustration nine

Manufacturers – Black, Black & Blackemore's , Salford

Cloudtanic later renamed Gondalus

SIDE ELEVATION

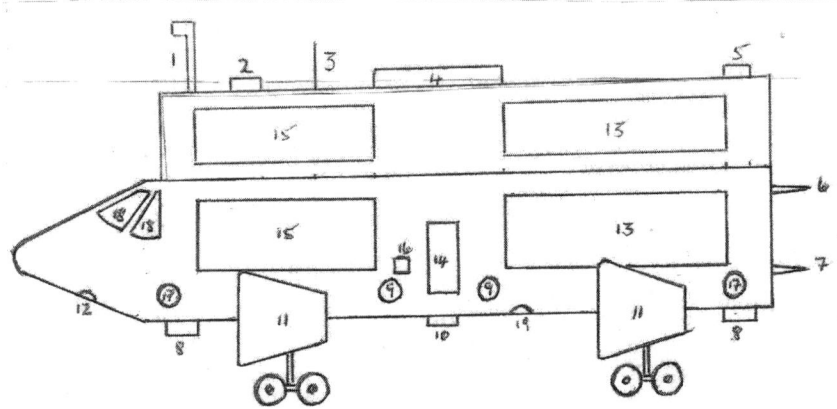

1. Periscope with TV camera which has infra-red capability to see through cloud.
2. GPS antennae (Global Positioning System).
3. VSI antennae (Vertical Separation Indicator – used in cloud formation flying).
4. Emergency parachutes.
5. Identification Beacon (every cloud machine has its own ID code).
6. Telephone antennae.
7. Radio Transmitter/Receiver antennae.
8. Atomiser – converts water into cloud by a process of evaporation (some water is stored onboard, some as ice).
9. Dispenser – converts stored water and stored ice plus cloud vapour into rain by a process of melting and condensing.
10. SOAKometer – early form of navigation aid with built in water location system.
11. Fan Duct Motor – propels cloud. A cloud has its own natural buoyancy.
12. Porthole for winch cable.
13. Saddle type water storage tank.
14. Side entry door.
15. Fuel tank for Fan Duct Motors.
16. Panel of buttons to open/close entry door and deploy/retract entry ladders.
17. Loudspeakers.
18. Cockpit window.
19. Fuel hose point.

Illustration ten

Manufacturers – Black, Black & Blackemore's , Salford

The Gondalus

INTERNAL LAYOUT OF TOP DECK

1. Stairs
2. Corridor
3. Crew sleeping quarters
4. Crew showers and toilet
5. Crew galley
6. Crew dining room and relaxation area
7. Passenger luxury gymnasium
8. Passenger shower and toilet
9. Passenger galley
10. Luxury passenger dining area
11. Luxury passenger lounge with bar, TV and PPI
12. Luxury passenger bedroom
13. Luxury passenger bathroom and toilet

Maps

Map one

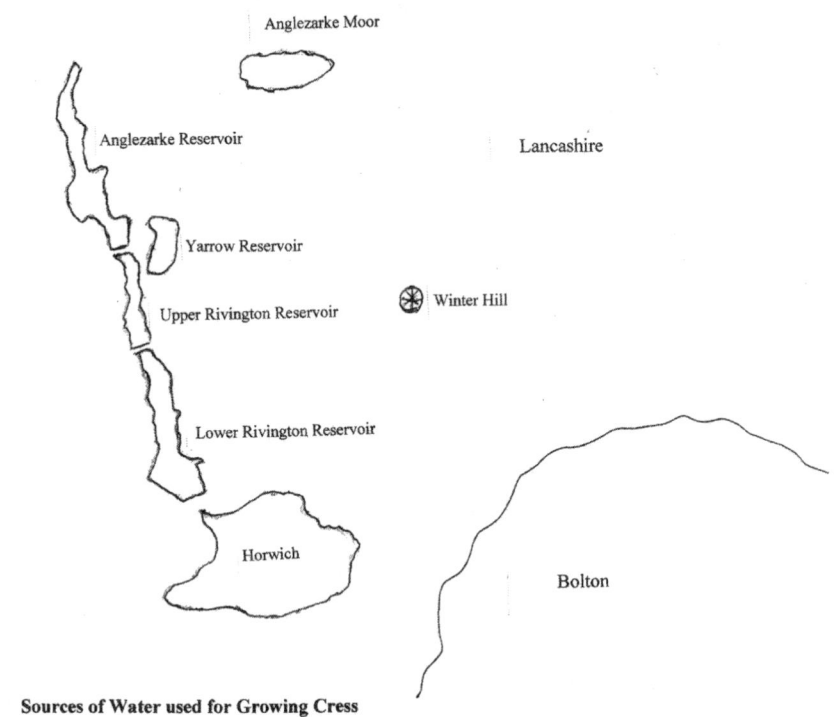

Anglezarke Moor

Anglezarke Reservoir

Lancashire

Yarrow Reservoir

Upper Rivington Reservoir

Winter Hill

Lower Rivington Reservoir

Horwich

Bolton

Sources of Water used for Growing Cress

Map two

Route of the Honeymoon Cruise by the Gondalus

1. Wythenshawe
2. Douglas, Isle-of-Man
3. Bangor, Northern Ireland
4. Campbeltown, Mull-of-Kintyre
5. Oban
6. Portree, Isle-of-Skye
7. Stornoway, Isle-of-Lewis
8. Wick
9. Banff
10. Arbroath
11. North Berwick
12. Berwick-upon-Tweed

Map three

Converging courses of the Nimbus and Discovery

1. Wythenshawe
2. Newtownards
3. Dublin
4. Kirkcubright
5. Peel

203